FIFTH-GRADE
FRANKENSTEIN

Also by Terri Fields:

Bug Off!

The Day the Fifth Grade Disappeared

Fourth-Graders Don't Believe in Witches

FIFTH-GRADE FRANKENSTEIN

TERRI FIELDS

AN
APPLE
PAPERBACK

SCHOLASTIC INC.
New York Toronto London Auckland Sydney

For Lori, Jeff, Rick, & Mom
who make the magic in my life
and
for all the students across the
country who wrote to me and asked
for a sequel to
*Fourth-Graders Don't
Believe in Witches,*
Mrs. Mullins is back with
another adventure.

ISBN 0-590-62368-0

Copyright © 1996 by Terri Fields. All rights reserved. Published by Scholastic Inc. APPLE PAPERBACKS and the APPLE PAPERBACKS logo are registered trademarks of Scholastic Inc.

12 11 10 9 8 7 6 5 4 3 2 1   6 7 8 9/9 0 1/0

Printed in the U.S.A.   40

First Scholastic printing, November 1996

1

"There's not gonna be any teacher here to-day!" Andy announced. Everyone in room 5C had been whispering, but we all stopped and listened. He went on. "No getting bossed around! No work and no books and NO tests today!" He smiled. "Let's party!"

"But what about Mrs. Evans?" Amanda asked, looking worried.

"Mrs. Evans isn't coming," Andy answered. "Because if she were, she'd already be here. Right?"

That was probably true. Mrs. Evans had never ever been late. In fact, she was always in our room by the time the first kid wandered in. Some of us wondered if she slept in the coat closet to get to school so early. And it *was* ten minutes after the tardy bell, and there still *was* no teacher in room 5C.

Jennifer stood up and tossed her long blond hair. "Okay, but even if Mrs. Evans is out today, I think we're probably going to have a substitute."

Justin grinned, showing off the missing tooth he'd lost in a fight. "Yeah? Then where is the sub? I think we've finally scared them all away. And you can thank me and Andy for that. It wasn't easy to do some of the stuff we did." He stood up and gave an exaggerated bow.

Jennifer giggled. "Like the time you put the snake in the sub's briefcase?"

Justin looked proud. "Yep, or the time I ate the worm right in front of the sub, and then I threw it up all over her lap. It was the grossest thing I've ever done!"

"But . . ." Amanda said, "even if there was no sub, wouldn't Principal Dugan come in? He wouldn't leave us without a teacher."

That left everyone pretty quiet. Principal Dugan definitely would make sure we had a teacher even if he had to come teach us himself. Then I had an idea. "Uh," I said, "maybe, no one knows that we don't have a teacher. Maybe they think Mrs. Evans is here."

I felt pretty proud of myself for being the first one in the class to figure that out, and then Jennifer turned around and hissed, "Allan Hobart, that's so stupid!" I could feel my face getting red. Jennifer was the most popular girl in the class, and when it came to me, she was also the meanest. I don't know why she hated me, but she never missed a chance to make fun of me, and she

2

sat right in front of me so she had lots of chances. My mom said not to worry about it because the kids who were really popular in elementary school weren't usually very important as adults. Somehow that didn't do much to make me feel better.

Justin shrugged. "Who cares why there's no teacher here. Let's just have fun."

Candice popped in, "We just need to make sure we don't go out of the room except at lunch and recess. That way no one will ever know."

Jennifer walked up to the front of the room and took a piece of chalk. On the blackboard was a whole section titled "Today's Assignments." She erased everything under it and in big yellow chalked letters, she printed, "Do whatever you want!"

For a minute everyone just sat there. I mean it was such an awesome thought that no one knew quite what to do. Then everyone started moving at once. Kate took out two big pieces of bubble gum, which was definitely against the rules, popped both in her mouth, and blew a gigantic bubble. Amanda got the art supplies and announced that she was going to paint all day. Jeff took his baseball out of his backpack and held it up asking who wanted to play. "In a while," Justin answered. "First, I want to go through Mrs. Evans's desk."

"I'll play ball," I said, but then Jeff could hardly

hear me because everyone was shouting.

All of a sudden, a huge boom even louder than all of us made us stop and watch the door to room 5C crash open. It hit the wall so hard that the glass almost broke. And, filling up the entire doorway was a man — or actually it may have been a monster. He sure looked like Frankenstein, except maybe Frankenstein wasn't as big or as ugly. The monster-man had to stoop to get through the doorway, and he strode into our classroom with huge, pounding steps. He wore black cowboy boots which seemed like they could stomp out a person. His jeans stretched up legs that went on forever, and huge muscles looked like they were going to burst right through the starched white shirt he wore. The guy's neck was bigger than most people's heads, but his face was the scariest thing of all. A huge black mustache drooped down like a big black frown. His eyes looked black too, and they scowled hatred. In all his terribleness, he stood in the front of the room, and he grinned showing a huge gold tooth. "I am your substitute teacher, and you have thirty seconds to get this room in perfect order and get in your seats or . . ." he glared at us, and hissed "or else . . ."

He didn't have to finish the sentence. We all flew back to our seats. "You," he barked at Bobby, "move faster, and when you get to your seat, get your hands folded on your desk." He made a fist and began pounding it into his other hand. "And all of you get your eyes up here on me, NOW!"

We were all staring so hard at this movie-monster of a substitute that practically no one noticed a little old lady in red sneakers had walked in behind him, and taken a seat in the back of the room. I might not have paid much attention myself except I knew that old lady very well. "Mrs. Mullins," the words just sort of popped out of my mouth.

The booming voice cut across the room. "I don't remember asking you anything. What did you say?"

"Me?" I asked stupidly. The substitute continued glaring. "I . . . uh . . . I just said 'Mrs. Mullins,' uh, the lady who is in the back of the room. That's her name."

Jennifer raised her hand. "I can tell you who she is; she's Allan Hobart's baby-sitter."

I could feel myself blush.

"Excuse me," came a rather scratchy voice. "But I certainly do not think of myself as a baby-sitter. In fact, I've never wanted to be a baby-sitter, and I definitely do not wish to baby-sit a class of fifth-graders. I happen to be a family friend of the Hobarts." All 4 feet 11 inches of her sat up a little straighter. "Furthermore, I certainly did NOT make the school rule about a mother being in the classroom with a substitute. It's Mrs. Hobart's turn today, and she couldn't come so I'm filling in for her. My name is Henrietta Mullins."

"Ma'am. Thank you, but I really do not need to know your name. I really do not need you here. You see I know I won't have any trouble handling this bunch of . . . of . . ." — he paused, and cracked every single one of his knuckles — "kids." He spat the word out like it was something disgusting. Then he turned his attention from Mrs. Mullins, stared at us and added with a steely tone in his voice, "Now for the rules. There is only one: I make all the rules. You follow them. Got it!"

Mrs. Mullins interrupted, "Excuse me again . . ."

But she never got any further. Our monsterman glowered, "I thought I made it clear. I won't be needing any help from you, so please be quiet. You can go home if you want, or you can just do your knitting in the back of the room, but you are to stay out of my way."

Mrs. Mullins folded her arms across her chest, and tapped one foot on the floor. She fixed him with a tight smile, and said softly, "I see." I recognized her tone of voice too well, and I sucked in my breath. I didn't care how big this guy was. He shouldn't have been so mean to Mrs. Mullins, and not just because it was rude to talk to little old ladies that way. He didn't know Mrs. Mullins or what she could do, but I did. I saw her reach for her purse out of the corner of my eye. I knew that if she had some of her magic powder in there, it was possible for anything to happen.

2

Come on, Mrs. Mullins. I hoped she'd catch my thoughts. *Come on! Turn this super-sized jerk into a dog or make our ten-foot Chocolate Man reappear and challenge this guy to a fight.*

I knew if I turned to look at Mrs. Mullins, the sub would probably kill me, so I closed my eyes, concentrating hard, trying to make her get my message. The next thing I knew there was this slam on my desk that made the whole thing shake. "This is not nap time!" The monster-sub leaned over and stuck his face in mine. "Even for little boys who bring their baby-sitters to school."

Jennifer laughed, and I felt like crawling into a crack in the floor and disappearing. I made no more effort to contact Mrs. Mullins. She'd have to decide to do something magic on her own.

Eyes forward, I watched the substitute pace across the front of the room. He looked like a caged lion. He hadn't told us his name — maybe he didn't even have one! Anyway, none of us were going to ask. He got busy issuing orders. "We will have spelling first today. Get out your spelling books. Make it fast." We started to get our books. "Faster!" he barked at us.

An evil smile escaped his lips. "Now, write each word in the review unit fifty times." There was a sort of group gasp at the idea. There were seventy words in this unit. That meant we were going to have to write 3,500 words today!

Jennifer Swanson, whose big baby-blue eyes had gotten her whatever she'd wanted almost all the time, was quick to raise her hand. Mr. Monster-Sub ignored her. But that didn't stop Jennifer. This girl was not used to being ignored. "Uhm, excuse me, please," she said. "I know it's hard to be a substitute for lots of different teachers, and I'm sure you do a great job. But you see, here at this school in Mrs. Evans's class, we always do reading first, and then, when we get to spelling, we do something fun like hangman. We never have to just copy words."

Having explained the way it should be, Jennifer smiled her little fake smile at Mr. Monster-Sub. It was sickening the way she worked, but she knew exactly how to butter teachers up. Jennifer always got her way with teachers. But, as much as I hated her, right now I was rooting for Jennifer all the way.

The class looked at Mr. Monster-Sub expectantly. Now that Jennifer had straightened him out, how would he change the assignment? He looked at us and didn't say anything. At first, we hoped that meant he was thinking about changing it, but the silence went on. Finally, Mr. Monster-Sub cleared his throat and in a voice that was very soft and super mean, he said, "I think I made my instructions perfectly clear the first and ONLY time I gave them." He hooked his huge thumbs on his belt loops.

I had a sick spot starting in my stomach, and I'm sure everyone else did, too. We were all thinking the same thing. If Jennifer, the girl that all grown-ups loved, couldn't get this monster-sub to listen, who could?

Then a scratchy voice from the back of the room spoke. "Excuse me again, but I really do believe that you and the children could compromise. Perhaps, they could write each word ten times for you, and then you could let them play hangman afterward."

Mr. Monster-Sub didn't even bother to look at Mrs. Mullins. He just stared at us and said, "Anyone who doesn't get started this second will have to write every word sixty times instead of fifty."

That did it. Thirty heads bent over thirty pencils, and we began to write. Pretty soon, my hand was aching. Lots of kids began shaking their arms or rubbing their hands, but none of us totally stopped writing. I began watching the clock.

Fifteen more minutes. Ten. Five. And then the best sound in the world, the recess bell. We gladly dropped our pencils and pushed back our chairs.

"Hold it," the substitute commanded. "Just where do you think you're going?"

"It's recess," Andy said, "and every kid gets to go outside."

"Is that so?"

Andy sat up a little straighter, like maybe the extra height would matter. But his voice didn't sound so sure when he said, "Yeah, we're definitely supposed to go to recess."

Mr. Monster-Sub crossed his arms and moved closer to the door. "I see. Whose words are all copied?" No one's hand went up. I mean, who could copy 3,500 words in that amount of time? The guy's huge head nodded, and his gold tooth shone as he smiled. "That's what I thought. Then we'll just have to skip recess today so you can finish your work. Keep writing."

"But that's not fair," complained Justin. "You can't do that!"

"Oh?" Mr. Monster-Sub glared at Justin, "And just why can't I?"

"Be . . . because teachers have to be fair."

Mr. Monster-Sub walked over to Justin's desk, and he put his face close to Justin's. "Life is not fair," he said in a loud whisper. "I am not fair, and if you don't get your words copied, you might just

11

have to miss lunch, too. Have I made myself clear enough for you, son?" Mr. Monster-Sub walked back to the front of the room, sat down, put his feet up on the teacher's desk, and looked out at us as if he was really enjoying our pain.

Through the window, we could hear the shouts of other kids playing basketball at recess. They sounded like they were in a whole different world. This substitute teacher was crazy, but I wasn't going to be the one to tell him so. Like the rest of the class, I just shook my aching hand and copied more words. We needed another adult to intervene. Mrs. Mullins! I shot her a desperate glance, and she mouthed, "I'll try."

A couple of minutes later, she walked to the front of the room. It was hard to hear her, but since I was sitting near the front, I could just catch her words. "I realize you're the teacher, but I think the children know that you're in charge now. Don't you think they're ready to go on to something else besides spelling?"

"Oh," he said, quite loudly. "Then you think I should give them the rest of the spelling words for homework?" The whole class gasped and shook their heads, and Mr. Monster-Sub looked at Mrs. Mullins. "Hmm, from what I hear, the students aren't in favor of that plan."

"That was not what I suggested, and you know it," Mrs. Mullins said firmly. With Mr. Monster-Sub sitting down, and Mrs. Mullins standing up, she was able to look him straight in the eye. The two of them stared at each other for a minute, and lots of the kids put down their pencils to see what would happen next. *Come on, Mrs. Mullins!* I encouraged silently. *Work a spell that turns him into an ant.*

Mr. Monster-Sub finally broke the silence. "As I understand it, you were to be here to help if the class was unruly or misbehaved. Since that is not happening now and WILL not happen later, you really don't have any role here, do you?"

The two of them were still staring at each other. Without breaking her gaze, Mrs. Mullins asked, "So that's how it is?" She went to the door of the classroom and walked out.

"Oh great," Jennifer Swanson whispered to me. "She turned out to be a *real big* help!"

"Just wait," I whispered back. "I'll bet she went to get the principal. She's gonna get this sub kicked out of here, and we're gonna be free!"

Mr. Monster-Sub walked over toward me. "Is there a problem here?"

"Uh, no, sir," I replied.

"I didn't think so," he said, and then softly under his breath he added again, "after all, any kid who needs a baby-sitter at your age . . ."

I hated him. I really did. I wished I could have been right next to Mrs. Mullins as she told the principal what was going on in room 5C. As much as I detested the thought of having a parent in the room, I was glad Mrs. Mullins had been here today. Principal Dugan might not have believed a kid, but I could just imagine what was going on as Mrs. Mullins was explaining this substitute. Principal Dugan was going to be mad. He was always saying how proud of Miller Elementary School he was and how great the teaching staff was.

I kept glancing at the door to see if anyone was coming, but I didn't see or hear anything. I guessed it was taking a long time for Mrs. Mullins to tell the principal everything. Jennifer whispered, "Your Mrs. Mullins probably isn't even coming back."

But I knew she was. She wouldn't desert us. Besides, her purse was still sitting in the back of the classroom. Meanwhile, I kept writing. My hand was aching so badly that my whole arm hurt, and I was still nowhere near finished copying spelling words. I'm sure everyone really wanted to stop writing, but even Justin and Andy, who almost never listened to anyone, were still working. There was just something about the way this guy said that life wasn't fair . . .

Finally, I heard footsteps, and I turned toward the door. This big old bully of a sub was going to get it now! The door opened, and Mrs. Mullins walked in. She looked at no one; she just headed to the back of the room, picked up her big black purse, walked back to the front and opened the classroom door. Every eye followed her, and there was silence as the heavy door shut behind her. Jennifer shot me a special look of disgust. I was pretty disgusted myself. Mrs. Mullins was supposed to be my friend. Mrs. Mullins was supposed to be magical. But without one word of explanation, she had deserted us and left us to the mercy of Mr. Monster-Sub. He grinned at us evilly. "I guess you all might want to work a little faster."

3

When the lunch bell rang, we were still sitting in our seats, copying words. It had been the longest morning of my life. Usually by the time the bell finished clanging, everyone was out of the classroom on the way to the lunchroom, but not today. I raised my hand. I didn't want to do it, but somehow, I felt I should. It seemed almost my fault that Mrs. Mullins who should have been the adult getting us out of this mess had left us to face it completely on our own. I waved my hand in the air. Mr. Monster-Sub was sitting at Mrs. Evans's desk. He was leaning back in her chair, and his huge feet were crossed on top of the desk. He glared at me over those big, black boots of his, but he didn't call on me. I took a deep breath. "Uhm, that's the bell for lunch. May we go?"

"Who's finished writing spelling words?"

Of course, no one had. No one could write that

many words in a morning, and he knew it. I raised my hand again. "We're all pretty hungry." For a second I thought I saw Justin look at me with awe. Then Mr. Monster-Sub's shoes clanged down off the desk onto the floor. *That's it*, I thought. *I'm dead. He's gonna come over here and kill me.*

He stood up, and he stretched. He was so tall that his hands almost reached the ceiling when he stretched. "I don't really care if you're hungry, but you know, I think I'm hungry," he announced. "If I could, I'd leave you in here working, but I can't leave you in here without a teacher, so you get lunch." The sound of relief filled the room. Then the sub continued, "But if any of you is even one second late from lunch . . ." he paused and stared at us. He didn't have to finish. "Now get out of here. I'm sick of seeing your faces."

We hurried to the lunchroom. It was hard to believe that it was the same old blue lunchroom and that everyone was acting as if it was a perfectly normal day when the truth was that the kids in room 5C had a monster for a teacher. Even though the girls in our class usually sat at one table and the boys at another, today everyone quickly gathered around one table. Kids started complaining at the same time, when Justin broke in with a shrill whistle. "All right, we don't have long. We've got to take this guy out. I say we all rush him after lunch."

"Rush him? Are you kidding? Have you noticed how big he is?" Candice said.

"Yeah, but if we all stormed him at one time . . ."

"Oh, yeah, right. Then we'd all be in big trouble. I don't want detention forever; I just want out of this classroom today." Jennifer rolled her blue eyes. "I'm going to see Principal Dugan."

"But I'm sure Mrs. Mullins already did that," I said.

"We don't know what, if anything, old Mrs. Mullins did." Jennifer looked at me, "Right, Allan?" Then she turned and headed out of the lunchroom.

"Well, I'm going to call my daddy!" Jamie said, and ran to catch up with Jennifer. "He won't like this at all!"

Justin looked a little deflated. "I still think we should just storm the guy." No one answered him. Instead, we pinned our hopes on the two girls leaving the cafeteria. Principal Dugan loved Jennifer. He thought she was the one perfect angel in our class, so maybe she could get through to him. And there was always Jamie's dad. According to her, he wouldn't put up with this sub for one minute. We watched them disappear down the hallway.

"Jeez, lunch is already half over," Joel complained, and we dug into our food. Suddenly, everyone realized that they were starved and couldn't talk anymore and still have time to eat. It was pretty quiet for the rest of the lunch hour — except for the sound of food being chewed. It was sure taking Jennifer and Jamie a long time to get back.

The bell ending lunch sounded, and Jennifer and Jamie came running back into the cafeteria. "Hurry," Candice shouted to them, "we want to know what happened, but we'd better not be late!"

"Well," Justin said, "what did happen?"

Jamie looked sheepish. "My dad's secretary said he was in an important conference and couldn't be disturbed."

Jennifer tossed back her blond hair, "Mr. Dugan is at some meeting at the school district office, and his secretary just said to be a good little girl and run along to class. Can you believe it?"

Justin groaned, "I can believe we're stuck with this guy for the rest of the day. Let's ditch!"

"Not me. No telling what he'd do if he caught us trying," Joel said. So everyone hurried back to class. Facing him was going to be bad enough without being late. I slid into my seat seconds before the tardy bell rang and hoped that the rest of the day was not going to mean more copying of spelling words.

It was probably stupid to hope at all, but I kept

wishing that lunch would make him nicer. Jennifer raised her hand.

"Yes," he barked.

"Uhh, I was just wondering if you had any ideas for our class science project."

"Class science project?" he snarled each word.

I'll say this for Jennifer. She didn't give up easily. She smiled so that her dimples showed. Teachers always thought she was cute. "Yes," she nodded as she spoke. "Principal Dugan announced last week that each class was to design a special science project this week. It can be on any subject, and the class with the best project will win a pizza party."

"Pizza party?" the sub thundered in disgust. "I don't care about a pizza party. "I don't like projects, and I really don't like to listen to kids talk." He thought for a minute. "Actually, I don't even like kids when they're quiet." Mr. Monster-Sub stretched and cleared his throat. "So we'll just skip working on any project for this afternoon." He paced back and forth across the front of the room, and we watched him walk.

Amanda gave it one last brave try. "Uhh, what did Mrs. Evans leave for us to do in her lesson plans?"

The substitute looked at her. "I understand this class never let the substitute follow the lesson plans that were left, so what difference does it make? I'll tell you what I've decided you'll do this afternoon." We all sucked in our breath. Who knew what terrible things his mind could think up next. If there was any more copying involved, I thought my hand would fall off. He spoke at first almost as if he were talking to himself. "We'll do . . . social studies."

I was relieved. No more copying spelling words. "Get your social studies books out now, and make it quick!" he ordered. Soon, a red book entitled *These United States* sat on all our desks — except Justin's. I saw him sneak his from his desk into his backpack. "Okay. I'm assigning each of you a different state. Read everything you can about the state and write a report. Oh, and make it neat and at least two pages. If the report isn't finished by the final bell, I'll just stay with you until it's finished. Now, get to work."

With that he gave everyone a state. I got Arizona. I was lucky. It didn't get to be a state until 1912 so there wasn't nearly as much to read as the people had who'd gotten a state like Maine or Pennsylvania. "You all better hurry," he announced before sitting down in his chair. Then he noticed that Justin had no book. He strode over to the desk, boots pounding against the floor. I wouldn't have wanted to be Justin. "Where's your book?"

Justin looked at him. "I don't know. I'm really worried about it. I guess it got stolen or something."

Mr. Monster-Sub hooked his thumbs in his belt. "I see. So that's how it is."

"Uh-huh," said Justin. "I'm really sorry. I don't want to cause any trouble, but I guess I can't do the assignment.

"Open your backpack."

"Huh?"

His huge frame cast a shadow over Justin's desk. His voice dripped with meanness. *"Open your backpack."*

Justin didn't move. I don't know whether it was because he wanted to defy Mr. Monster-Sub or because he was frozen to his chair with fear. I do know that the guy reached down and grabbed Justin's backpack. He picked it up, unzipped it, and held up the book for the class to see. No one moved. No one breathed. "Well apparently, you don't think books belong on desks, but you do think they belong on the floor. Fine. Have it your way. Come with me." When they got to the front of the room, Mr. Monster-Sub put the book on the floor and commanded Justin to stand on it. "You'll stay that way until school is out, or it will be my personal pleasure to meet with you after school."

So much for taking the guy out. Justin looked thoroughly miserable standing in front of the class. I counted the pages in the chapter on Arizona. There were nine. Great. Read nine pages and do a two-page report before the end of school. Didn't anyone tell this guy that you weren't supposed to have to finish the year's course in social studies in just one day?

The room was totally silent. We didn't even bother moving when the afternoon recess bell rang. What was the point? We just tried to shut out the sounds of kids having fun. The afternoon dragged on. Every minute seemed to take forever but even so, we knew time was moving too fast to get all the work done. Mr. Monster-Sub obviously never heard of the idea that school could be fun — especially at recess.

I really don't know how we all did it, but somehow everyone got their reports done with five minutes to spare. We watched as he had us pass them up the rows and then he took the whole pile of papers in one huge hand and slapped them on the teacher's desk. Thank goodness we had only three more minutes until the final bell — not enough time for any more torturous assignments. We were watching the clock big-time now. We were counting down. Two more minutes until the final bell. It had been the worst day of school any of us had ever had, but at least it was almost over. With any luck we'd *never* get this guy back again as a substitute. Who had ever thought that it would be great to see Mrs. Evans?

The substitute cleared his throat. It seemed he had a parting shot for us, but we didn't care. He was out of here. "Oh, by the way," his obnoxious voice rang out, "Mrs. Evans may not be back this whole week. So understand this. Today, we didn't get much done; tomorrow, you'd better come prepared to really work!"

"Not a whole week," I heard Andy gasp, and then the final bell rang. School was out for the day, but our terrible troubles were just starting.

4

Everyone trudged out of the classroom. A week with Mr. Monster-Sub was way beyond anyone's worst nightmare. As we started down the hallway to the front door of the school, Andy poked me and said, "Everyone in five-C meet by the tree in the front. Pass it on." I told Jamie who told Candice who told Justin, and pretty soon it looked as if the whole class was headed for the big oak tree on the lawn in front of the school. As soon as we got there, Andy took charge. "No way are we going to put up with a week of Mr. Monster-Sub. We need a plan!"

"I'm telling Principal Dugan," Jennifer said.

"You already tried that, remember?" Andy rolled his eyes.

"Well, this time I'm staying in the office until I can talk to him. Who's coming with me?" Most of the class followed along.

"My goodness!" exclaimed Mr. Dugan's secretary. "What's going on? School's out. What's everyone doing in the office?"

"We really need to see Mr. Dugan," Jennifer said. "It's so important," she begged.

"Yeah, and we're not leaving until we do," Justin added.

"I see, well, let me buzz him." The secretary picked up her phone, and the next thing we knew, Mr. Dugan came out of his inner office.

About ten people started to talk all at once, and Mr. Dugan held up his hand for silence saying he couldn't understand anyone. As soon as it was quiet, Jennifer explained why we shouldn't have this substitute ever again. She told the principal every terrible, gory detail about our sub, and she ended by saying, "I knew you'd want to know everything right away. That's why I came to tell you even before I went home today."

Principal Dugan scratched his head. "Well, I do thank you for coming in. Let me just see if I understand everything. It seems that you must have learned spelling really well, and I know that's important. You got behind in your work this morning, but since you didn't want extra homework, the substitute allowed you to stay in during recess and finish. This afternoon you learned about all fifty states. As a matter of fact, the substitute dropped the reports off to me on

26

his way out. I must say, I was impressed."

"But you don't understand at all!" Justin exclaimed.

"Oh, but I do, Justin. Up until Mr. Masters came to substitute today, no sub this year had ever agreed to come back to your class for a second day. But Mr. Masters has even agreed to be here for the whole week, and he told me that you were no problem; he had things well under control. He said he wouldn't need any parent helpers. That meant I was able to call the next parents on the parent patrol list and tell them they didn't have to come." Mr. Dugan looked at Jamie. "Actually, it was your father who was due in tomorrow, and he was absolutely delighted that we'd found such a wonderful substitute.

"So I appreciate your all coming in, and my door is always open to you, but I think it makes sense to have Mr. Masters back. After all, you're learning, and class behavior is good. That makes me happy, and I know it will make your parents happy."

When you explained things that way, Mr. Masters Monster-Sub sounded perfectly okay. So, we were doomed, and we knew it. We weren't going to get any help from the principal. We weren't going to get any help from our parents, and thanks to Justin, we'd already seen what happened to anyone who tried any tricks to lighten the load. The awful truth was that it seemed as if we couldn't beat this guy, and we couldn't get rid of him either.

"Well," Jamie said, "I'm still going home and tell my dad. Mr. Dugan just didn't explain it to him right. Wait and see; my dad'll do something. I know he will!"

Justin fiddled with his baseball cap. "Yeah. Much as I don't like getting my mom and dad anywhere near school, I think we'd all better go home and talk to our parents. We've got to make this guy out to be so bad that Mr. Dugan hears from every one of them tomorrow. You know Dugan . . . enough complaints and the guy will go."

So we all agreed to go home and basically just tell the truth about this guy. He was bad enough that lies weren't necessary. I thought about stopping at Mrs. Mullins's house to ask her why she had deserted us, but I was still pretty mad at her, so I decided to skip it. Instead, I went directly home and worked on the best way to get my mom on my side against my substitute.

When Mom came home from work, I waited until she had a little time to get dinner. I offered to help with stuff, and then right as we were finishing, I told her all about Mr. Masters. She listened and shook her head. "He certainly doesn't sound very nice; it's a good thing he isn't your regular teacher."

"That's it?" I questioned.

"What's it?" she replied.

"Aren't you going to do anything about him?"

"Well . . ." she hesitated. "When you grow up, sometimes, you'll have to work with very unpleasant people. At least give it another day or so Allan, it will get better. Besides, I have an important client coming in tomorrow. I've got to be there."

"But Mom . . ."

Unfortunately, she got one of those looks on her face that meant she didn't plan to discuss it any further. I went to my bedroom to think. I hoped that other people's parents were doing their jobs to stick up for their kids because I knew my mom certainly wasn't going to be any help. Jeez, I'd failed my class twice. First Mrs. Mullins wasn't any help, and now my own mother.

I trudged to school slowly the next day. I was probably the only one who was going to arrive without a furious parent. But when I got to school, there was good news and bad news. The good news was that I was not the only jerk without a parent to help get rid of Mr. Masters. In fact, it turned out that none of our parents had come through. Jennifer did get her mother to call Mr. Dugan, but when her mom hung up the phone she told Jennifer that Mr. Dugan was monitoring things and had everything under control.

For all Jamie's promises about her father, all he had done was to say that a little discipline never hurt anyone.

Day two with Mr. Monster-Sub was even worse than day one, if that's possible: no morning recess and impossible assignments that were the absolute example of how to create a horrible school day. Then, at lunch, Andy dared Justin to throw a spit wad at the sub. Justin was actually dumb enough to take the dare, and when he got caught, Mr. Monster-Sub made him stand on his tiptoes and press his nose to the blackboard. Then Mr. Masters drew a circle on the board where Justin's nose hit the board. "Now, you *will* keep your nose in this circle for the next fifteen minutes, or you *will* spend one hour with me after school." Poor Justin had to keep standing on his tiptoes the whole fifteen minutes. By the time he was done, his legs were shaking.

When the last bell finally rang, we trudged out of the classroom. Three more days with this monster of a man was more than any kid should have to bear. No one even had any plans or ideas. Everyone just straggled home, feeling beaten.

As I walked, I tried to think things out. *Was this guy really that impossible?* I asked myself.

Yes, definitely! Then why was it that no one was willing to help us get rid of him? I couldn't figure it out at first. Then I thought about it a little more. It had to be that when our parents heard about him, his assignments didn't seem so bad, but if they could actually just be there to see him in action . . . then they'd believe us. But he'd taken care of that. Just when the parent patrol finally could have really been some help, he'd gotten rid of it. It didn't seem as if any adult was going to set foot in our classroom to see the truth of what a monster this guy was! Then it hit me. One adult already had. Mrs. Mullins! Instead of heading home, I made a right turn and headed directly for her house.

I pressed the doorbell again and again. Mrs. Mullins opened the door out of breath. "My goodness, where's the fire? I was clear out in back. Give me a chance to get to the door! Come on in. I was just trying a little something in my sewing room."

Trying a little something usually meant she was working on a little magic, and normally, that would have been pretty great, but not today. Nothing, not even magic was going to get me off the subject. I glared at her. "Okay, Mrs. Mullins, why'd you just desert us yesterday?"

"Desert you . . . why whatever are you . . . oh, you mean leave school?"

I folded my arms. "Uh-huh. Exactly. You — you — walked out on us."

Mrs. Mullins tapped one sneakered foot and looked down the hall. "Why don't you come into the sewing room, and we'll talk while I work?"

31

"No. Let's talk about it right now, right here," I said a little strongly. I guess I was a little stressed out by the past two days. "I just want to know one good reason why you left us with that terrible substitute."

Mrs. Mullins sighed. "Allan, I'm truly sorry if I upset you. At the time, leaving seemed like the best thing for me to do. However, if I ever have to be on parent patrol again for your class, I won't leave. Okay? Now, do come in. I'm delighted that you're here, but I'm very busy with what I think will be a most wonderful concoction." She turned and walked into her living room as if the whole thing was a done deal.

I followed her in. "Mrs. Mullins," I said, "you knew how bad that sub was . . ."

She turned and looked at me. "Allan, for heaven's sakes. I said I was sorry. Now can we get on with things?"

"No, Mrs. Mullins, we can't! I need to know why you deserted us. I told my whole class not to worry, that you'd handle things, and you just walked out. What kind of friend does that?" I crossed my arms and stood up tall.

Mrs. Mullins sat down on the sofa and ran her hand through her gray hair. "Okay. I can see that we need to talk." She motioned to me to sit down. "First of all, I didn't just walk out on you. I left the classroom because it appeared that anything I said was going to be used by the substitute to make your lives a little more miserable. You do remember that when I suggested you'd had enough spelling, his response was to threaten to make it all homework. Right?"

I nodded. "But . . ."

Mrs. Mullins stopped me. "Let me finish. After I left your classroom, I didn't just leave the school. I went to the principal's office to let him know that I felt the substitute was being unfairly difficult on all of you. Principal Dugan then explained to me everything that your class had done to substitutes, and well, my goodness, Allan, you all should be ashamed."

"That really wasn't me . . ."

Mrs. Mullins held up her hand. "At any rate, the principal said that your class was a disaster when it came to subs, and no one wanted to substitute for you all. He was glad to have found this man, and he wasn't concerned if you had to work a little harder. It would only make up for work you hadn't done when other substitutes were there."

"But Mrs. Mullins, this guy is awful! You shouldn't have left us with him," I said, trying to forestall a possible lecture about how your behavior always comes back to you.

Mrs. Mullins dusted a speck on the coffee table with her apron. "I left because I felt my staying was only going to antagonize your substitute. Besides, I figured maybe your principal was right, and it wouldn't hurt your class to get a mean substitute yourselves for one day — especially since you've been so mean to all of your substitutes."

"Yeah, well it wasn't just one day." I explained everything that had happened since she left. "And so, he'd going to be our sub for at least the rest of this week and maybe even part of next week, too."

Mrs. Mullins's eyes grew large, and she shook her head. "Hmm, a week is a very long time, and I'm afraid that man really is not a nice person at all."

"Yeah, you can say that again. But the worst part is that no matter how awful he is to us, he makes everything he's done come out sounding okay to grown-ups." I told her about Jamie's father and about Principal Dugan. "You're the only grown-up who understands. Can't you, like, use some magic so the next time he starts to say something mean he'll just turn into a really little kid?"

I liked that idea a lot. I could just imagine what Andy and Justin would do if he was half their size.

Mrs. Mullins stared at me and folded her arms. "Allan Hobart! Now just what do you think would happen if I walked into your class and turned your teacher into a small child?"

I pushed my baseball hat back on my head.

"Uhhh . . . we'd all be really happy and really grateful to you?"

Mrs. Mullins tapped her foot angrily. "Wrong answer. In no time at all, everyone would know my secret. I might as well stand on a roof and shout, 'Ladies and gentlemen, I am a witch — a kindly one who only tried to help your children — but a witch nonetheless.' " She tapped her foot even faster. "Now, you tell me, what would happen after that?" She didn't wait for me to answer. "We both know. I'd be forced out of town. I don't want to move. I love it here. How would my secret ever be safe if a whole class of fifth-graders watched me perform a spell?"

"Okay, okay," I agreed. Mrs. Mullins stood up and began pacing the living room, and I could see how upset she was getting. I put the thought of a seven-year-old Mr. Masters out of my head. "Well, maybe, you could just call a meeting of all our parents and explain what the monster-sub is like."

Mrs. Mullins shook her head. "Allan, Principal Dugan already knows about the situation and if he's happy, I suspect your parents will be happy, too. I'm afraid you're just going to have to do the best you can to get through this week."

"Yeah, but it's not just any old week. Friday night is the school's science fair. Our class wants to win so bad. Mrs. Evans promised us that if we did all our work last week, she'd give us every afternoon this week to get the project done. The winning class gets a pizza party. Now everything, and I do mean everything, is ruined! Not only that but my fingers have blisters from writing so much" — I rubbed my hand — "and we haven't had recess at all. I think this guy may kill us with busywork before the week is over. Mrs. Mullins, please. You've just got to do something! Please. I'm asking you as my friend. You're our only hope. Won't you help?"

5

Mrs. Mullins walked over to me. She was wearing a green-flowered dress, and when she walked, she looked kind of like a round flower garden. She smiled at me, "Oh, all right. When you put it that way, how can I refuse?"

I grinned. "Yes! I knew you'd come through. Now, what are we gonna do?"

"I don't know, but I certainly am glad to see you feeling better." Suddenly, Mrs. Mullins put her hand to her mouth. "Oh, dear me, my work. I've gotten so caught up with you and your substitute, I almost forgot. I hope everything is still okay." She hurried down the hallway, and I followed quickly behind her.

"What are you trying to do?" I asked. "And how come you're doing work in the sewing room? You always work in the kitchen."

"True," she said, opening the door to the sewing room, "but since I'm making a new dress, I thought I should do it in the sewing room."

"Making a new dress?" I was confused. "I thought you were working magic."

She giggled. "Making a new dress is magic for me. I don't know how to sew at all."

"Oh." I tried to hide my disappointment. I'd been in the sewing room a couple of times before, but it had never held much interest. There was a big old-fashioned sewing machine in the corner. Maybe making a dress was magical for her, but I was hoping for *real* magic.

Mrs. Mullins rushed over to a small desk next to the sewing machine. I hoped she'd get this dress finished fast so we could talk about our monster-man substitute and what to do about him before I had to go home for dinner. Then I looked around the room again more carefully. There was no material in here. There was no partly finished dress. There was only some neon-pink powder in a little jar on the desk. Suddenly, things looked much more interesting. "So, uh, Mrs. Mullins, tell me about this dress."

She held up the powder. "Do you like this color?"

"Yeah, it's fine, why?"

"Do you think it looks good next to my skin?"

"I guess so. I don't know much about stuff like that, but it's a real nice color. It's bright."

"I thought so, too. I thought it would be just perfect for Jane Lockwood's tea this Saturday."

Mrs. Mullins buried her head in the big magic recipe book on the desk.

I thought Jane Lockwood was just an uninteresting old lady. I didn't know quite why Mrs. Mullins wanted to waste time going to her tea, and I said so.

"It's kind of like your wanting to play baseball with a friend. I think this tea will be fun." Then she stuck her head back into the black book. "Hmm," she said, "this recipe says that once the proper color has been obtained, the mixture should sit for five minutes." She looked at me. "How long do you think we were in the living room talking?"

"I don't know. It didn't seem like very long at all."

"Okay," she said, "then maybe we're still on track. The problem is that there's a big splotch right here on this page of my magic book, and I can't quite read what it says to do next. Come see what you think."

I leaned over the page, thinking for a minute of all that we had done to rescue the big black book. It was too bad that it had so many holes, tears, and spills, but we had been lucky to get it back at all. I tried really hard to see the words in the place she pointed, but there was a big black smudge of something on the page right in that spot. "I think it says to add . . ." I stared again. "I don't know. I can't tell what it says to add."

Mrs. Mullins ran her hand through her gray hair. "Oh, and I so wanted this dress to be perfect for the party. What could I still need to add?" Mrs. Mullins scurried from the sewing room into the kitchen and the cabinet marked SPICES. There she pushed aside the spice rack and stared at rows and rows of labeled MAGIC POWDERS. "Ah, maybe a little of this! What do you think, Allan, one tablespoon or two?"

"Well, Mrs. Mullins, what exactly are we going to do?"

"We're going to create a perfectly wonderful bright pink dress for me to wear to Mrs. Lockwood's party. And when I get a compliment, which I surely will in the dress I'm about to whip up, I can honestly look at all those lovely ladies, and say, 'Thank you so very much, I made it myself in my sewing room.' " Mrs. Mullins giggled.

I had to admit that even though I had no interest in dresses and even less in tea, it was going to be fun to see Mrs. Mullins make the dress of her dreams magically appear.

"So . . ." Mrs. Mullins said carrying the powder back to the sewing room. "Look at the recipe book again. Do you think it says one tablespoon or two?"

I stared hard at the page. I just couldn't tell. "I don't know. Use two. One might not be enough to make the dress show up out of nothing."

Mrs. Mullins cocked her head, thought for a moment, and said, "All right. That makes as much sense as anything, and since we can't read what it says . . ." she stopped talking and scooped two tablespoons of the white powder into the pink, then stirred the mixture well. She held it up to the light. "That should do it. Now, Allan, since you're here, you can help me."

"Great!" I said. I loved helping with any kind of magic stuff.

"I'm going to stand right in the center of the room and recite the spell. You're going to take the pink potion and pour it slowly over me. Make sure that it covers me completely so the dress will be the right size." She handed me the small jar, and suddenly, I felt nervous. I know it was just a dress we were conjuring up, but still, Mrs. Mullins was all excited about it, and I didn't want to do any magic wrong.

She began to chant:

"A vision of pink, I want to be.
A vision of pink for all to see."

As she chanted, I poured slowly making sure that I walked around her in a circle as I poured. In no time, the jar was empty, and she had stopped chanting. I stood back ready to see her in her new pink dress. Nothing happened.

41

"Maybe it takes a few minutes," I said.

"Maybe so," she replied. "Well, let's start talking about your substitute while we wait."

"Great!" I said, but I could see that she was not thinking about my substitute at all. I saw her look across the room at the mirror and bite her lip. The dress should have appeared by now. "I guess maybe I waited too long to finish the spell."

I felt bad. It was my fault she'd waited too long. "Hey, Mrs. Mullins, you could always start the whole thing over again. The party isn't until the weekend, and I'll help you get everything ready."

She smiled. "Allan Hobart, you are a nice person and a good friend. And you're absolutely right about this. We'll just start the whole thing again from scratch tomorrow. But right now, we're going to work on doing something about your monster of a substitute."

I really appreciated Mrs. Mullins more than ever, and I promised myself that as soon as we took care of Mr. Masters, I'd help her create a spell to make the most perfect dress this town had ever seen. I could see she was upset even though she was trying not to show it, because her face was very pink.

"Come on," she said, "let's go in the kitchen. We'll have some lemonade, and we'll think about what we can do with your Mr. Masters."

I walked out of the sewing room in front of her, and I headed into the kitchen. I went to the cupboard to get some glasses for our lemonade, and when I turned back around, I yelled, "Yikes, Mrs. Mullins, are you okay?"

"Yes, Allan, of course, I'm okay. I mean I wanted the dress, but we'll try again tomorrow. What's wrong with you?"

"No," I sort of croaked. "It isn't me. Mrs. Mullins, uh, why don't we kind of just sit down."

"Allan, what's going on?"

I pointed to a chair. I knew she'd better be sitting when I told her. In fact, I wasn't sure I could tell her at all. It might be better to show her. "Don't move. I'll be right back," I said. "Just sit there and wait."

I ran down the hallway to the sewing room and grabbed the hand mirror I had seen there. Then I ran back to the kitchen. "Allan," came her panicked voice. "Look at my hands!" There was a frantic look on her face. "Uh, Mrs. Mullins, it isn't just your hands." She grabbed the mirror from me and held it up to her face. The reflection that stared back was pink, not just any pink, but the brightest, most shocking, most neon pink I had ever seen. Even her gray hair was no longer gray. It, too, was shocking pink. Only the very tip of her nose was its normal color. She looked like one of the Saturday morning cartoons come to life.

"Oh dear, oh my, oh dear," was all she kept saying over and over.

I didn't know what to say at all. "Uhh, it'll probably wear off, won't it?"

Mrs. Mullins was still staring in the mirror. A big tear rolled down her cheek. "Allan, I made the color permanent so that my nice new dress wouldn't fade in the wash." Her eyes darted from the face in the mirror to her hands. Then she put down the mirror and pushed up the long sleeves of her blouse. Her arms were brilliantly pink, too. Pulling up her long skirt just above her high-topped red sneakers showed a little bit of shocking-pink leg. "I, uh, I seem to be this bright pink from head to toe." There was a catch in her voice. "How will I ever go out of the house again?"

I didn't have an answer to that, and I watched in disbelief as she continued to get even pinker. Soon, her skin was so blindingly shocking pink that it almost hurt to look at her. Her hair was brighter pink than the drummer's in the punk group Scrunge. The neat little bun looked so strange. Hair as shocking a pink color as Mrs. Mullins's definitely needed to be spiked up high on the head of a guy with tons of tattoos. It did not belong on this little old lady!

Mrs. Mullins was definitely right about one thing. If anyone saw her like this, she would be the talk of the town forever. She definitely couldn't go out. But Mrs. Mullins couldn't stay hidden away forever, either. I needed a quick solution to this mess of a problem. If only I'd let her finish her spell before I'd insisted on telling her my problems, Mrs. Mullins might have had her dress, and I would have had a solution to Mr. Masters.

I took my baseball hat off and put it on backward. Sometimes, that helped me to think. I looked at her. "Okay, Mrs. Mullins, you're always telling me not to get so upset about things and to believe more in myself. So . . . I believe . . . I believe that . . . that there must be some other spell to undo what we did. We'll just have to find it."

Mrs. Mullins was sitting at the kitchen table with her very, very pink elbows on the table, and her shocking-pink hands were cradling her extraordinarily pink face. "Well, maybe," she said. "I've never heard of such a spell, but I guess anything is possible."

"Hey, you'd never heard of a spell that turned people colors, but now you know one, so let's get going on that magic book!" I was determined to keep us thinking on a positive note.

We walked back down to the sewing room. Mrs. Mullins was so bright that she almost seemed to glow. Together, we looked in the index of the magic recipes, but there was nothing about turning people back to their original color, maybe that's because there was nothing about turning them different colors in the first place. By the time we'd gone over the index to magical recipes twice, it was starting to get dark outside. I just couldn't figure out how everything had gone so wrong. Pretty soon, I was going to have to go home for dinner, and I didn't have any kind of solution to Mrs. Mullins's pinkness or Mr. Masters' meanness.

Mrs. Mullins and I both sat in the sewing room thinking, but the only brilliant thing in the room was the color of Mrs. Mullins's skin and hair, and they just kept getting brighter and brighter. Now even her eyes glowed neon pink. And just as I was thinking that nothing worse could possibly happen, there was a knock at the door.

6

"Be very quiet," she whispered, "and maybe whoever it is will think I'm not home."

I nodded. But there was another knock, and then the doorbell rang. "Henrietta, if you're in there, answer the door. If not, I'm going to call the police. I know I heard noise in that house, and if the person I'm speaking to is a robber, well then you'd better know that you're dealing with the president of our Block Watch Association, and I take my job *very* seriously!"

"Oh, no, Miss Switzer," I whispered. "She'll never just leave." I couldn't believe our bad luck. This lady had been driving us crazy for a year. She lived next door to Mrs. Mullins, loved gossip, and was always looking for something really shocking to add to her knowledge of the town.

"Allan, you'll have to answer the door. We don't want her calling the police, and we definitely can't let Miss Switzer see me!" whispered Mrs. Mullins.

"What'll I say?"

The doorbell rang again. "This is your last chance, robber. I'm going to call the police. Henrietta, if you're there and tied up, don't worry. I'll get help!"

"Go," Mrs. Mullins hissed, "now!"

I went to the front door, but I had absolutely no idea what I was going to say. Why would I be in the house if Mrs. Mullins wasn't? And if Mrs. Mullins was here, why couldn't Miss Switzer see her?

I took a deep breath and opened the door. Blanche Switzer glared at me. "You? What took you so long to open the door? And where's Henrietta? Well?"

"Well, uh?"

"Speak up, young man. You're being rude. Answer my questions. I'll just come in and have a seat while you go get Henrietta. Now run along."

I knew I couldn't let her in the house. I stayed right in the entrance. "But . . . uh . . . Mrs. Mullins isn't here right now."

"She isn't?" Miss Switzer stuck her beady little face toward mine. "Then may I ask, young man, what you are doing here?"

"What am I doing here?"

"Don't repeat what I've said. Answer me. I think there's something very strange going on in this house." She pointed her finger at me. "You know I've thought there was something unusual here ever since Henrietta first moved in."

"Strange . . . ah, no there's nothing strange at all," I said, thinking of the shocking-pink Mrs. Mullins in the other room.

"Then where is Henrietta, and why are you here if she isn't?"

"That's a very good question, and uh . . . well — " Suddenly, an idea popped into my brain. "You see, I wasn't supposed to say because she wanted it to be a surprise."

Miss Switzer looked pleased. "Oh, that's okay. You can tell me her secret."

"Uh, no, I don't think I'm supposed to do that."

Miss Switzer smiled at me, and her voice dripped with fake sweetness. It was enough to make me barf! "Why, Allan, you know that it's important for children not to keep secrets from adults, especially, policemen, right?"

"Policemen?"

Miss Switzer stood tall. "Well, I am the president of the Block Watch Association, and that's almost like a policeman."

I forced myself not to laugh. Let her think she'd convinced me. "Well, okay, but don't tell that I told you."

"Oh, I won't!" she exclaimed. "I never tell secrets!"

Except to the whole world, I thought to myself. "Well, the secret is that Mrs. Mullins is making a very special dress for a tea she's going to on

Saturday. I was visiting her when she realized that she had run out of thread to finish the dress, and so she uh, she ran to the store."

"Oh," Miss Switzer looked interested.

"And just what color is that dress."

"Pink," I said, "definitely pink, but she doesn't want anyone to know that."

"Excellent," Miss Switzer clapped her hands together. "You really aren't quite such a horrible child after all. Well, be careful here. Don't destroy anything, and you don't even have to bother telling Henrietta that I was here."

I shut the door and leaned against it. That had been a close call. "Well done, Allan, that was really fast thinking!" Mrs. Mullins said. "Give that woman a bit of gossip and she's just got to go share it! We won't see her again tonight. Now that we've gotten rid of her, we've got to get me back to normal, and I've been thinking. What if we just followed the exact same formula except this time, we tried for my normal flesh color? I'll call your mother at her office and ask her if you can stay for dinner so we can get right to work."

"But Mrs. Mullins, you were trying to make a dress, not dye your skin. If you do the spell again, won't it make the dress?"

"I don't think so. We'll just make exactly the same mistakes we made the first time."

In no time, my mother had been called and had given permission for me to stay for dinner, and we had all the powders out to start the spell again. Mrs. Mullins had started to hum while she got the magic powders ready, so I didn't think it was a good time to mention that she was rarely able to work a spell the same way twice. That was one reason our magical adventures never turned out exactly the way we planned. But this time, the plan just had to work because neither of us could think of anything else to try. She stirred and mixed, and finally, she turned to me. "Okay, now for the color part. Do you think this looks like flesh?"

"Not exactly, I think it looks kind of orange," I said staring at it carefully. "Wait a sec. I have some crayons in my backpack. I'll see if there's a flesh color." There was and I brought it to Mrs. Mullins.

"Hmmm," she said, "you're right. This mixture is much too peachy. I don't want to go from shocking pink to orange. I just don't know how to get this fleshy color. Maybe, I could just dissolve your crayon into our mixture to get the color right."

"But won't that change the spell?"

"I don't think so. It's only color, not a magic ingredient. You don't mind losing the crayon, do you?" I shook my head no. The next thing I knew the crayon had disappeared into the mixture. "Now, we just have to wait. I was just to this point when you came in. So let's go in the living room and talk. Then we'll come back, add two tablespoons of IYTNM powder, and work the spell!"

We went into the living room. It was pretty dark in there, and Mrs. Mullins was glowing. Once I'd had a glow-in-the-dark baseball, but I'd never seen a whole glow-in-the-dark person! I tried not to stare.

"As long as we're waiting," I said, "maybe we could talk about Mr. Masters. How about if we turned him some awful color. Maybe, he'd get so embarrassed that he'd just have to leave."

"Possible," said Mrs. Mullins, "but you do have to have a substitute teacher, and you don't have anyone else who wants to do it, so maybe it would be better to make Mr. Masters nice than to make him disappear."

I didn't think any magic could make that man nice. I didn't even think he was human. Mrs. Mullins and I discussed some possibilities. I was all in favor of having him disintegrate in front of the class, but she wasn't interested. We talked a little more, and then Mrs. Mullins said, "Well, I think it's time to finish this spell. Let's get me back to normal, and then we'll deal with Mr. Masters."

We went back to the sewing room and added the two tablespoons of IYTNM powder. I picked up the mixture. It didn't look powdery like the last one. It looked kind of rubbery. "Uh . . . Mrs. Mullins," I said.

"I know. I know. Maybe, we just need to pour it on quickly. I'll start the chant. You start pouring, and we'll both start hoping."

Mrs. Mullins handed me the jar. She began to chant:

"A vision of flesh, I want to be.
A vision of flesh for all to see."

I started to dump the mixture over Mrs. Mullins, but it wouldn't come out of the jar. I shook it and shook it, but the mixture didn't move. Spying a spoon on the desk, I grabbed it and wedged it in the jar to pull the mixture out. Yanking as hard as I could, I suddenly felt the goop dislodge, and then before I could stop it, the stuff turned into a ball, and bounced its way across the room.

"Oh, no," Mrs. Mullins cried. "There goes my skin color!"

I ran after the ball, scooped it up, and whispered, "I hope this is right." Then I pitched the ball right at Mrs. Mullins. It was a great pitch; my baseball practice must have been paying off! It hit her perfectly. Then the stuff started to spread out. My mouth fell open as I watched the goop begin to cover her skin. It was like a paintbrush. Her hands then her arms turned flesh-

53

colored. Then her neck and her chin turned back to her normal color again. "It's working!" I shouted to Mrs. Mullins. "We did it!" I grinned.

Mrs. Mullins had pulled up her long skirt enough to see that her legs above her high-topped tennis shoes had also turned back. "We certainly did!" she smiled.

My smile disappeared. "Uh . . . not quite," I said. "Uh . . . Mrs. Mullins, your hair is flesh-colored, too."

She looked in the mirror. Her face was its normal color, no more glow-in-the-dark pink, but she was a strange sight. I'd never seen anyone whose hair was the exact color of their skin. She looked a little like one of those alien creatures on *Star Trek* with the gigantic heads.

"Gosh, I'm so sorry," I said. "I really thought the spell had worked. Now what?"

But to my surprise, Mrs. Mullins didn't seem too upset. "Well, I'll just have to change the color of my hair."

"Do you know a spell for that?"

Mrs. Mullins smiled. "Uh-huh, and this one is fail-proof. It's called hair dye, and it's found at the drugstore. You know before my hair turned gray, it used to be brown. I think I'll just dye it back that way."

"And no one will suspect that you were doing magic?"

Mrs. Mullins laughed. "No, Allan, lots of

women dye their hair every day. Tomorrow morning, I'll just put on a scarf and go down to the drugstore to buy some hair dye. Now, let's discuss your problem with Mr. Masters while we have some hot dogs for dinner."

I put lots of catsup on my hot dog, and Mrs. Mullins added a little relish to hers. I didn't realize how hungry I was. "I still think," I said between mouthfuls of hot dog, "that we need to do something to make the guy disappear."

"And I still think," Mrs. Mullins said, "that that does not address the problem of your needing a substitute."

"You could be our substitute."

"I don't think so. That job isn't for me. Let's work on Mr. Masters."

I took another large bite of my hot dog and thought, *Okay, if you won't disappear him, why not make him smaller than all of us? Remember, I talked about it before. If you just shrink him, then we'll still have a substitute, and he will think twice before being such a bully.* I could see the whole thing. It would be so neat. Just before the spell went into effect, I would look at Mr. Masters, Monster-Sub, who had even terrified our two famous troublemakers, Andy and Justin. And I would walk right up to him in front of the whole class. Then I would put my hands on my hips, give him my most disgusted look, and I would say, "You are a big bully, and I am not copying any more spelling words — not today, not tomorrow, not ever again." The whole class would be staring at me. They'd think I was the bravest person in the whole world. But then that awful monster-sub would reach out toward me with those giant hands. The class would gasp, sure I was going to be killed, but suddenly, the guy would start to shrink. He'd look confused, then scared. I'd still be standing there facing him. Pretty soon, I'd be able to look at him right in the eye. But he'd keep shrinking. Smaller and smaller he'd get until I was looking down at him, his puny little hand still outstretched. I'd reach out and push his hand away. "And another thing," I'd say, "this class needs to work on our class project, so that's what we're going to do." Boy, everyone would want to be my friend. No one would ever forget Allan Hobart's facing down the meanest substitute in the whole world.

"Allan! Allan!" Mrs. Mullins's voice interrupted my daydream. She sighed deeply. "Allan, have you heard a word I'm saying? You're not thinking. Can you imagine what a scandal it would start if the man walked into your class one day so tall that he had to stoop to get through the door, and the next day, he was shorter than all of you? I don't know if I even could do such a spell, but even if I could, I wouldn't. Don't you remember the giant daisy you created? We had news stations, newspapers, and lord knows what else. Can you imagine what would happen if word got out that a teacher had shrunk in front of the class?"

"Kids everywhere would think you were a hero," I replied.

"Wrong. Scientists and snoops from everywhere would come here to learn how it had happened. Allan, forget it. The idea is out of the question. Besides, I still think the best thing to do is just to try something to make Mr. Masters nicer. He's already scared you all to death. I think even if he was nice now, everyone in your class would behave, and you could get your class project done. Best of all, no one would suspect me of doing any magic."

I had to admit that I was disappointed. I wanted to watch the monster-man shrink. But Mrs. Mullins had made her point. There was no way that she was going to make our sub pint-sized, so the next best thing was to at least make him nicer. "Okay," I said. "So how will it work?"

Mrs. Mullins patted her flesh-colored hair. Her hand blended right in, and the whole thing looked so silly that I had to bite my lip to keep from laughing. "Actually," she said, "I'm not sure yet just how I'll make him nice."

"Maybe you could give me the potion, and I could work the magic. That way you wouldn't even have to come to school!" Another brilliant idea. I'd never gotten to make magic on my own, and I'd been watching Mrs. Mullins for almost a year, and I was sure I could do it.

Mrs. Mullins shook her head. "Oh, Allan," she said, clearing our plates from the table, "I thought you understood by now. Only witches can work spells. Our magic powders don't do a thing for anyone else. Now tell me, if we can get Mr. Masters to let you do it, what is this project your class plans to use to win the fair?"

"Uh, well, uh, actually, we haven't exactly got one."

"Haven't got one? How can you be sure you'll win a prize if you don't even have an idea what you want to do?"

"Well, it isn't as dumb as it sounds. See Mrs. Evans said we'd pick a project on Monday, and we'd work on it every afternoon for the rest of the week. Only now Monday and Tuesday have both passed, and we haven't gotten one minute to come up with a plan. The whole class has been too busy just trying to survive to even think of the perfect science fair project."

She tossed me a dish towel, and I dried the dishes she'd washed. "Then I'll tell you what," she said, "you go home and think about a great science fair project, and I'll stay here and plan a spell to improve Mr. Masters's disposition." She put the dishes I'd dried in the cabinet next to the magic potion cabinet.

"Oh, I want to know what it is. Can't I at least

look in your magic book with you before I go home?"

"All right," she relented. "Now where did I leave that big thing? You'd think such a big book would be hard to misplace."

"The sewing room," I interrupted. "Remember?"

"But of course," she said. She quickly bustled to the sewing room. We had to be so careful turning the pages of the magic book. It was very old, and it had been through a lot.

"Wow, a spell to turn someone into a frog! I thought that stuff was just in fairy tales. Hey, we could turn . . ."

Mrs. Mullins fixed me with a stern stare. "Don't even think about it."

At last, we found a spell to improve disposition. Not only that but the recipe wasn't smudged or torn or anything. The whole thing was there clear as could be.

"Excellent!" Mrs. Mullins said. "I think this will do nicely." She perched her granny glasses a little farther down on her nose and began to read. "Okay, uh-huh," she said to herself. "Perfect. Perfect. Then if you blow a little of the M8%GN solution on the person, the next word you say will be the way the person acts for a week."

She smiled at me. "So, how about that! We even have the perfect spell. Now you quit worrying. Go home, do your homework, and I'll be at school first thing in the morning to put my magic into gear. I'll see you there."

"But Mrs. Mullins, your hair?"

"Oh, dear me. I almost forgot. Well I'll have to take care of that first. But I'll be at school just as soon as I get my hair a normal color." She walked me to the front door. "See you tomorrow." She glanced up in the sky and smiled. "Oh my, look at the ring around the moon. Isn't that wonderful!"

"I guess so," I said.

"Why, don't you know what that ring means?" I shook my head no. "Oh, Allan, sometimes I forget how much you still have to learn. That ring means tomorrow's going to be a powerful day for magic."

7

It was a good thing that I didn't have much homework to do, because I just couldn't concentrate at all. I finally gave up and just went to bed. But I had trouble sleeping because I was trying to think of possible class projects and trying to figure out what everyone was going to say when Mr. Masters suddenly turned into Mr. Nice Guy. I tried closing my eyes really tight, but they flew back open.

I was really glad when it finally got light outside. In no time, I was up, dressed, and wearing my best good-luck Cubs hat for the day. My mom came in to wake me and could hardly believe it. "My goodness, Allan. What's going on? Could this be the same boy I practically have to drag out of bed every morning? What makes today so special?"

"Oh, nothing, Mom." She started to fix me with one of her mom looks, and I thought I'd better head it off fast. "Well, okay. I felt bad that I got home from Mrs. Mullins's so late last night, and I thought I'd get up early so we could have breakfast together."

Mom's eyes actually welled up. "Why, Allan. What a sweet thing. You are really one terrific kid."

Okay, so I hadn't exactly told the truth, but I did like having breakfast with my mom. Once we were done, I practically ran to school. By the time I got to the playground, I was grinning. It was going to be such an awesome day. Jennifer Swanson was sitting on the steps of the school. "How come you look so happy today?" she asked.

Usually, I would have just ignored her since she seemed to specialize in making mean remarks to me, but today I answered her. "I just have a feeling that today is going to be pretty terrific."

"Oh, yeah, another day with Mr. Monster-Sub. It figures that you'd like him. You know, Allan, you're even dumber than you look. And that isn't easy." Two of her friends who were sitting near her giggled.

I felt like sticking out my tongue at her, but instead I just said, "Okay, fine, you laugh now, but later, just remember what I said about it's turning out to be a terrific day." I opened the door to the school and headed toward room 5C.

If such a thing was even possible, Mr. Masters turned out to be even meaner than he had been the day before. "Alisha," he barked. "Front and center." Poor Alisha was the shiest kid in our class. It was torture for her even to ask a question, and everyone knew it.

"Me?" she whispered.

"You! Now!" he ordered.

Alisha rose from her desk, and she looked as if she were going to cry. By the time she was standing in front of us, I think any one of us would have volunteered to take her place. She stood in front of the class, and her knobby freckled knees shook. Mr. Masters boomed, "Now recite the fifty states as fast as you can. I'll time you. If you can't do it in three minutes, the whole class will write the states five times each." The guy probably stayed up nights thinking of ways to torture kids. He took out a stopwatch. Of course, Alisha was much too terrified to even say one word. The three minutes ticked off in absolute silence, and then we all began to write lists of the states. The terrible quiet of the room was broken only by Alisha's sobs.

Okay, I thought to myself. Mrs. Mullins could show up any time now. Mr. Masters had made it quite clear the way the day was going to run. Still, time trudged on, and there was no Mrs. Mullins. At 10:00, I told myself that it must be taking her longer to color her hair than she'd planned. At 11:00, I told myself she would be bringing the magical potion at any moment. At noon, I went to lunch wondering if somehow Mrs. Mullins had forgotten that she was supposed to be here today. As if things weren't bad enough, Jennifer Swanson and group walked by me. "There's Allan," she whispered as I took the first bite of my sandwich. She spoke just loud enough so she was sure I'd overhear. "Remember, this torture is his idea of a terrific day." She rolled her eyes. "What a dweeb!" Her friends groaned. I put my sandwich down. Suddenly, I wasn't very hungry anymore.

After lunch, Mr. Masters started explaining about a book report that he wanted written. Justin raised his hand. He hated to read, and I was sure that he was going to try to get the assignment changed. Mr. Masters ignored him. Justin waved his arm in the air to make Mr. Masters notice. I decided that Justin was either very brave or very stupid or probably both. The monster-sub walked over to Justin's desk. He towered over him. "Listen, son," he hissed, "let me give you a little friendly advice. It's rude to put your hand up when someone is talking. Besides, if I wanted to hear from you, I'd ask. Now you put that hand down or else. Got it?"

At that moment, the door to the classroom opened. Just when I'd been about to give up hope, Mrs. Mullins stuck her head into the room. She looked very different with brown hair. Every eye in the classroom was trained on the door. We were all thrilled for someone, anyone to interrupt this master of misery. But I was the only one who knew how truly wonderful Mrs. Mullins's presence would be. "Excuse me," said her slightly scratchy voice. "I'm terribly sorry to disturb you, but it's imperative that I speak with you for just a moment."

"You again?" Mr. Masters thundered. His eyes swept down over her in disgust. "I thought I made it clear that I didn't need help handling things here."

"Oh, you did that quite well," she admitted, "but I do need to speak with you for a moment. It won't take long at all."

"You'll have to wait. Come back after school. I'm teaching, and considering that this class knows nothing, I don't have time for you now."

Mrs. Mullins sighed. "Very well." She opened the door a little wider and entered the classroom.

The monster-sub was over near her in only three big strides. "Just what do you think you're doing?" He was so tall and she was so small, that her eyes were just a little higher than his belt buckle. Nonetheless, she tried to look him in the eye.

"Well, I walked here, and at my age, I'd be much too tired to walk home and back again at the end of school. So I'll just have a seat in the back of the class, and I'll wait until after school or whenever you say it's best to talk to you."

The class was fascinated, and I was so proud. Mrs. Mullins wasn't letting this giant jerk intimidate her one bit. He looked at us, and a scowl crossed his face. "Get back to your work," he ordered.

None of us had the guts to remind him that he hadn't finished giving us an assignment. He looked at Mrs. Mullins. "See how you're disrupting things. These kids can't concentrate with any distractions in the room." He stroked his big, black mustache. "All right, lady . . . step outside. You've got one minute to let me know what's on your mind. Then you go out the front door, and I go back in the classroom. Got it?"

Mrs. Mullins actually smiled at him. "Quite so. And I thank you in advance for your time."

The two of them walked out of room 5C, and I wished more than anything that I could follow them out. I knew just what was going to happen. I wished I could watch. Mrs. Mullins was going to take that little bubble blower on the chain around her neck and gently blow its magic potion at Mr. Masters. Then she had to fix her eyes on him and firmly say NICE. That was all there was to it. Mr. Masters would return to us a truly nice person for a whole week. It was going to be awesome!

"Well, isn't it?" I felt a nudge in my back. "Hey, I'm talking to you." Candice said.

"Huh?" I turned in my seat to face her.

"That's your baby-sitter, Mrs. Mullins, isn't it?" she asked.

"Not my baby-sitter, our family friend," I corrected.

"Well, whatever. It's wonderful that you got her here. No one else in the class got a parent to come in." Candice looked at Jennifer and Jamie.

Justin chimed in, "Good work, Hobart. The longer Masters is gone, the less work he can give us. I just hope she can keep him out there for a while. What'd she want anyway?"

Just then we heard a terrible noise in the hallway. Mrs. Mullins appeared in the doorway; her glasses were hanging half off her face. Mr. Masters must have done something awful. He was even meaner than anyone could ever imagine. He was three times as tall as she was and ten times as strong. "Are you okay?" I said jumping up from my seat.

"Allan," she said to me, and there was panic in her voice. "Your project — the one for the science fair, well . . ." her voice rose higher and sounded even more frantic. *"It's gotten loose."*

"My project?" I said in confusion. "Uhh . . . what project? I still haven't thought of any . . ."

Mrs. Mullins interrupted. "Allan, now!" she commanded. "Come right now, and bring a couple of the strongest boys with you. We can't keep this project from the class any longer can we?" She sounded very determined.

"No, I . . . I guess not." I had no idea what was going on.

Justin and Andy were already out of their chairs. If there was adventure, they wanted to be in on it. I couldn't figure out what was going on, but I knew something had to have gone terribly wrong. All three of us rushed to the classroom door. Other kids in the class started to get up. I didn't know what we were going to find, but I was pretty sure that the fewer people who saw it the better. "Stay here!" I commanded. I don't know where I got a voice that sounded like that, but everyone sat down. "We'll be right back." Andy, Justin, and I burst through the door into the hallway. At first we didn't see anything unusual. We didn't even see Mrs. Mullins. Then a voice called, "Over here, under the stairwell. Quick!"

"Awesome!" Andy shouted.

"Wow!" Justin chimed in. "Look at the size of that thing."

"Uh . . . uh . . ." I couldn't seem to say anything at all.

Mrs. Mullins locked her eyes into mine. "Boys, this is Allan's project for the science fair. The container has broken, and we must get this into water right away."

Justin's eyes were huge. "But where are we ever going to get something big enough for *this*? What happened to the bowl? How'd it get loose?"

"Young man, I think you need to stop asking questions, and help us start finding answers," Mrs. Mullins said firmly. "We must find a container and find one immediately."

There was a flapping sound on the floor. "I think that fish is dying," I whispered.

8

"Water!" Andy said. "We've gotta get water!" Then he ran to the drinking fountain, cupped his hand and ran back to the fish. By that time, there was only a little water left in his hands, and just a few drops splashed on the fish.

"Well, that was dumb!" Justin said.

"Oh yeah? You got any better ideas?" Andy shot back.

"Don't argue! We've got to save this fish!" Mrs. Mullins was practically in tears. "Now think," she ordered. "There must be something in this school that could be filled with water immediately."

"Maybe we should go find the janitor," Andy offered.

"No!" I said. "We don't need to find the janitor. We just need to get in the janitor's closet. He must have buckets for cleaning." Andy, Justin, and I took off down the hall in a run.

"If Mr. Masters sees us, we're dead!" Justin said as he sprinted.

I didn't even want to think about that.

"Did you see the teeth on that fish?" Andy said. "I never saw such sharp teeth except on a killer shark!"

We pulled open the door to the janitor's closet. "Look! A bucket!" Andy yelled. He didn't wait for me or Justin. He just grabbed it and ran toward the boys' bathroom to fill it with water. I wished I'd seen it first. So did Justin, because he looked down the hall and said, "That bucket will never be big enough anyway."

I could still see Mrs. Mullins at the other end of the hallway. Even though she was partly hidden behind the staircase, I saw the fish flopping around on the hard green floor at her feet. I hoped Andy would hurry. Even a bucket that was too small would be better than nothing at all. I started to shut the janitor's closet door. "Wow! That's it!" I half whispered aloud.

"What's it?" Justin said.

"Look!" I pointed to an old-fashioned bathtub. It was leaning upright against one wall. It had big bronze feet on it. I walked into the closet to try to push the bathtub out. Justin tried to pull from the other end. The thing was really heavy, but we finally got it out of the closet, and we laid it down so it looked like a regular bathtub.

"Fantastic!" Justin said. "Now let's just carry it down to the fish." We started to pick up the tub from either end. It didn't budge. Justin looked at me. "Too bad you're not stronger."

Yeah, right. I hadn't seen his end getting picked up either. Andy leaned out of the boys' bathroom. "Hey, come help me carry this bucket. It's heavy when it's filled with water."

"I'm coming," Justin said, and he shot down the hallway. Three of us couldn't carry one bucket, so I watched as the two of them got the bucket to the fish and plopped it in. I could see that part of the thing was still sticking out of the bucket. I tried to think. The bathtub would definitely be better, but if the bucket was heavy when it was filled with water, once we filled this bathtub with water, no one would be able to move it any place. In fact, even empty, we couldn't move it unless there were a lot more people carrying it. And we couldn't leave it here in the middle of the hall. Principal Dugan would flip out. I went back to the classroom. Just outside the door, I saw Justin and Andy arguing about who got to keep the fish. Mrs. Mullins was looking at me with pleading eyes. I could see she didn't know anything about how to handle those two. No one did, but at least I was thinking of a plan for the fish. I walked into room 5C, and I said, "We are supposed to walk down the hall in two straight lines and carry a bathtub from the other end of the hall into our class. There's to be no talking or . . ."

"A bathtub?" Candice said. "Are you kidding?"

"I knew it," Jamie said. "I just knew it. We have a psycho for a sub. What's he want a bathtub for?"

"Well that's absolutely it." Jennifer huffed. "I am not moving any bathtub into this class, and I . . ."

"Now!" I said. "We've got to hurry." I opened the door and marched out like I knew what I was doing. I hadn't told them Mr. Masters ordered us to get the tub, but if they wanted to think that, it would only get the job done faster. Actually, I wasn't even quite sure where Mr. Masters was. Maybe, Mrs. Mullins had made him so mad that the mean man had stormed out before she could ever start her spell. Still, if he was around someplace and he caught us all out in the hall, we were dead. I wondered if he had gone to the office to tell Principal Dugan to get Mrs. Mullins out of his hair or to complain that she'd brought a fish to school. And I wondered how she'd happened to have ended up with this strange fish.

While I was worrying about Mr. Masters, the kids in my class actually stood up and followed me out the door. They were listening to me! It was a pretty neat feeling. I just hoped I wasn't leading them into the monsterness of Mr. Masters. I'm sure any other class in the world, including ours (before Mr. Masters), would have

73

been laughing their heads off at the idea of carrying this big dumb old bathtub. But after a few days with the monster-sub, everyone just quietly held on and carried one part.

In no time, we had the tub in the room. Much to everyone's amazement, Mrs. Mullins, followed by Andy and Justin, walked in with the bucket and dumped the fish and the water into the tub. Everyone crowded around it and stared. "Well, don't just stand there," Mrs. Mullins said. "We've got to get more water into this tub or this fish will certainly die."

"But . . ." Jennifer started to say.

"No buts . . . let's get going with the water!" Mrs. Mullins ordered. For such a little lady, she could give pretty big orders! The kids took turns going to the bathroom in pairs, filling the bucket up, and dumping more water into the tub. This fish didn't look very friendly, but everyone who was standing around the tub cheered when the water was finally high enough for the fish to swim back and forth.

The cheer started everyone talking and then kids' questions were flying everywhere, and it was the noisiest I'd ever heard our class. I edged my way closer to Mrs. Mullins's ear and whispered, "You've got to get it quieter in here. If Mr. Masters comes back and finds us like this . . ." I drew my finger across my throat.

Mrs. Mullins looked at me. She started to say

something, but her voice wasn't very loud, and the noise was too much.

"Huh?"

Again her lips moved. Her voice was drowned out by Jennifer Swanson yelling, "OOOOOH, did you see the mouth? Look at those sharp teeth. I think it might be a shark."

Two girls screamed.

Things were out of control. Mrs. Mullins moved right beside my ear. "Whistle," she commanded.

"Now? Here?"

"Yes, right now!"

I put my fingers in my mouth and out came my longest and best whistle. It was my Allan-you-are-grounded-if-you-make-that-terrible-noise-inside whistle. By the time the noise of whistle had stopped ringing in my ears, I realized that I was hearing the sound of silence.

"Very good," Mrs. Mullins said, pushing her granny glasses back on her face. "Now that we've solved the immediate crisis, I will try to answer your questions. However, first you must all go sit down and be quiet."

Everyone went to their seats, but no one was quiet.

"I have a question!"

"No, I get to go first!"

"I get the first question."

"I got more water than you. I get the first question."

Mrs. Mullins looked at me. I wondered if Mrs. Mullins had ever gone to regular school or if they'd had a special one for witches. I raised my hand just enough so she'd see it but no one else would notice.

She looked relieved. "Quiet!" She tried to shout, but it was still kind of scratchy. "If you have a question, then you'll just raise your hand. I'll call on you one at a time."

Every single hand in the class went up except mine. I figured I'd wait until we could really talk. Mrs. Mullins's eyes swept the room, and then she pointed to Jennifer Swanson. I was disappointed. Mrs. Mullins was a witch. She should have known better than to choose dumb Jennifer first like regular people did. "Well, gee, I have so many questions," she said, trying to draw out her minute in the spotlight.

Mrs. Mullins scratched her head. "All right, then let's begin with someone who has only one easy question." Every hand shot up again. People were waving their fingers or stretching their arms to try to get her attention. Mrs. Mullins looked a little confused. "I'll tell you what. Maybe we shouldn't start with questions. Why don't I just explain what happened, and then if you still have questions, you can ask."

Every single kid's eye was on Mrs. Mullins. There was absolute silence. Even if the end-of-school bell sounded at that minute, I don't think anyone would have left class. Mrs. Mullins pushed her granny glasses up on her nose and wiped her hands on her dress. Suddenly, I remembered that Mrs. Mullins hated to speak in front of people. One time, at a witches' convention, they'd wanted her to give a talk on how to grow ice-cream trees, and even though the recipe had been invented by Mrs. Mullins's great-great-grandmother, Mrs. Mullins was too embarrassed to explain it to such a large crowd.

Now she stood in front of our whole class, and they were waiting for her to explain everything. Poor Mrs. Mullins, but I had to admit I was pretty curious myself. "Uh . . . well . . . actually, it's a very simple story." She looked over at me. "You see, Allan told me about your class project, and he said you really wanted to win, but you hadn't had any time to work on it." She paused.

"So, how does that explain this fish?" Andy demanded.

"The fish?" Mrs. Mullins said. "Well, ah . . . the fish . . ." Mrs. Mullins looked at the fish and then everyone else stared at the big tub. I wondered if the fish was going to talk for itself. I was the only one who knew that with Mrs. Mullins anything was possible.

Justin shifted in his chair. Then Mrs. Mullins's scratchy voice broke the silence. "Well, you see the fish was Allan's contribution to your class project."

My contribution? What was going on? Everyone turned to look at me, and I could feel the hot redness starting up my neck and across my face. Now my dumb freckles were really going to stand out. Everyone started asking me questions at once.

"So . . ." Jennifer said.

At that minute, I wished I had not ever suggested that Mrs. Mullins come to school. I had no idea why this fish was here or how much longer we had until Mr. Masters returned to this room and blamed everything on me. Then suddenly, I had this awful feeling. I told myself it just couldn't be. It was impossible.

"So . . ." Jennifer repeated again. "Allan, do you know why you brought this fish to school or not?"

I took a deep breath. This was not good. How could I know why I brought the fish to school, when I didn't even know there was a fish at school. I looked at Jennifer. I could tell she was about to let go with another put-down, so I blurted, "Of course, I know why I brought it."

"Well . . ."

"Well," I tried to think. I looked at Mrs. Mullins. I was stumped. "You know, Mrs. Mullins, since you brought this fish here for me and everything, why don't you tell 'em," I said.

The corners of Mrs. Mullins' mouth turned up just slightly, and she shrugged a little. Then she sighed. "All right. It's like this. Allan knew you wanted to win the science fair, and he knew that your substitute wasn't giving you any time to work on it, so . . ." I could tell she was trying to think of what to say next. "He decided to try to help the class out. He found this rather extraordinary fish. Now, he didn't want you to get in trouble with your substitute and, of course, none of you wanted the substitute to give you any more work."

"That's for sure!" Justin said. "I wish the guy would disappear forever."

"Shh," Jamie said, "let her finish the story."

All eyes watched Mrs. Mullins. "So," she paused a second. I wondered if I was the only one who could tell that she was making this story up as she went. "So, he asked me to come and talk to your substitute, to see if he would be nice enough . . ."

Jennifer jumped right in, "to let us work on the project. I know just what happened from there." She folded her arms smugly. I thought, *Good. Let her make up the story.* Mrs. Mullins and I were having a terrible time telling it. Mrs. Mullins probably couldn't tell what really happened, and I didn't know.

Jennifer continued, pleased to have everyone's attention. "Even nerdy old Allan figured that if he brought in an amazing enough thing, the sub would have to let us work on the project, but he was too scared to bring it in himself, so he had his baby-sitter do it!"

"Not true!" I defended myself. The next words just sort of popped out. "The sub would never have even let me get through the door with that fish. But I figured he would at least have to listen to an adult. So I asked Mrs. Mullins to talk to him."

"I kinda hate to ask this," Jamie said, "but just where is Mr. Monster-Sub?" She pushed her red pencil through her long dark hair. "I mean the last time we saw him, he walked out the door with Mrs. Mullins." All of a sudden, she got this real hopeful look on her face. "Oh, Mrs. Mullins, did you really get rid of Mr. Masters for us?"

Mrs. Mullins began to tap nervously on her chin with her fingers. "Good heavens, child, why would you think I could get rid of anyone?" Her voice had risen, and there were two rosy spots on her cheeks.

Justin laughed. "Oh, we know you couldn't really do anything to him. But what'd you say to him?"

"Well," she calmed down a little. No one knew anything. "As you remember, I asked him to step out in the hall for a moment, and he did. I started to tell him that I thought he should be nicer to all of you, but he did not like my interrupting him or your class, and well, he uh . . . he left!"

Everyone began to clap and cheer. The monster-sub was gone. Justin jumped to his feet. "Hey look at me. Who does this remind you of?" He stood on top of his desk and made his fingers droop around his mouth like a long mustache. Kids laughed. Still standing on the desk, Justin told Mrs. Mullins that she didn't need to tell anyone about our sub leaving. "We'll just take care of ourselves tomorrow! Me and Andy'll be in charge."

"I want to help!" Jennifer said. She stood up. "I'll help be in charge."

Mrs. Mullins looked at Justin and Jennifer. "But all children need teachers." She sighed. "I'll simply have to go to Principal Dugan and explain that you may need a new substitute for tomorrow." Everyone groaned. "Besides," Mrs. Mullins said, "someone has to teach you what to feed this fish. Does anyone even know what kind of fish this is?" There was a silence. Mrs. Mullins tapped her foot and looked concerned. "It's a piranha. Now, how can you win the school's science fair if you can't keep it alive?"

Before anyone could make a comment about that the bell rang ending Wednesday. Kids picked up their backpacks and filed out by the bathtub so they could get another look at our fish. I stayed behind. I wanted to know the truth about the fish. I didn't know what that truth was, but I did know that I had never mentioned anything about bringing in any kind of fish today.

9

I looked around our class. The room was completely empty except for Mrs. Mullins, me, and, of course, the fish swimming in the bathtub. Mrs. Mullins sat down in the teacher's chair. It was so funny to see her there. I couldn't imagine Mrs. Mullins as a teacher. I walked over to her full of questions. "Mrs. Mullins?"

She held up a wrinkled hand. "Not now, Allan." She seemed to be almost talking to herself as she said, "Heavens, but I'm exhausted." She pushed herself up out of the chair and walked to the door. "I suppose the only fair thing to do is to at least tell Principal Dugan that he'll need a new substitute for tomorrow."

She walked to the office. I followed. I wondered if Principal Dugan was going to be angry with her for making Mr. Masters so mad that he left. I wondered if principals could assign adults detention. Probably not. At least I sure hoped not. After all, Mrs. Mullins was only trying to help me.

"Hey, Mrs. Mullins, maybe Mr. Masters'll just come back tomorrow." I hoped not, but it seemed like the right thing to say.

"He won't be back tomorrow." She said it with certainty. I heard her take a deep breath as she turned the handle to the door marked PRINCIPAL'S OFFICE. Amazing. Mrs. Mullins' sigh was exactly the same as the ones the kids of 5C took right before we got called to the principal's office. I saw her approach Principal Dugan's secretary and then the door shut behind her. I figured I should wait outside for her. It was the least I could do. I crossed my fingers and hoped that Principal Dugan wouldn't be too upset about losing his substitute. In just a few minutes, Mrs. Mullins was back. I took that as a good sign.

"Well . . . ?" I asked.

Mrs. Mullins didn't say anything.

"Well, what happened in the office? Was Principal Dugan mad? What'd he say? And what happened to Mr. Masters? And what happened to the spell? Didn't it work? And . . ."

"Allan Hobart, enough! I have had all the questions I can take for one day!" She walked toward the front door of the school. "This has been quite an afternoon. I'm going home and make myself a cup of strong tea."

"Can I come if I don't ask any questions?"

Mrs. Mullins turned her head and looked sternly at me over her granny glasses. "I believe that was another question!" Then the corners of her mouth twitched up in just the smallest of smiles. "However, my friends are always welcome in my home."

The playground was deserted by the time we walked out of the school, and even though I was dying to ask Mrs. Mullins lots more questions, I bit the inside of my cheek to make myself stop. I knew Mrs. Mullins pretty well now, and I knew that if I didn't push her, she would tell me everything. We walked home without talking. Only the sound of our sneakers hitting the sidewalk broke the silence.

I glanced at her red sneakers and smiled. Before she'd met me, she'd worn these black, awful-looking, lace-up, old-lady shoes. I'd convinced her that sneakers would be much more comfortable. After she'd tried them, she'd agreed. So I told myself I wasn't always just causing her more work, sometimes I solved stuff for her too.

Once we got to her house, she walked past the cupboard with all the wonderful potions in it and opened one filled with ordinary kitchen stuff. From it she took a cup and a tea bag. "You can help yourself to some milk," she said, "and I think I have some brownies in the bread box."

I got my milk, and as I opened the bread box to get a brownie, I remembered the day we'd tried to create a spell to make brownies, but instead of the edible kind, we'd ended up with a puppy named Brownie right in the middle of the kitchen table. That had happened a whole year ago. It was the first time I really understood how amazing Mrs. Mullins was.

I got my milk and brownie and sat down at the kitchen table waiting for Mrs. Mullins. She sat down and took a sip of her tea. "What a day! And I didn't get one single thing done about my dress for the tea."

"Well, there's always tomorrow!" I said.

"Indeed," she replied.

I couldn't stand it any longer. "Aw, come on, Mrs. Mullins, tell me what happened!"

She took another long sip of her tea, pushed her granny glasses up on her head, and pursed her lips. "It was all supposed to be so easy. I knew exactly how to do the spell. I had the absolutely correct formula for the magic potion. And still . . . look at what's happened."

She picked up her blue cup and took another sip of tea. I forced myself to take a bite of my brownie. Was she ever going to get to the point? I decided to help her along. "So, you got to school okay . . ."

She nodded. "Yes, that part seemed to go just fine. I was a little late because I had to dye my hair, but I did get there. And although Mr. Masters was very put out with me, he did agree to step outside and speak with me for a moment if I promised I'd never interfere in his classroom again." Her hand fluttered up to the necklace. "So we stepped outside. He told me to state my piece and be gone. So I didn't even try to make small talk. I undid the little bubble-blower necklace around my neck, and I drew it toward my face. Then just as we'd planned, I said, 'Mr. Masters, I do believe that when it comes to dealing with children, you've simply got to be . . .' "

I interrupted. "Then did you sprinkle the potion on him?"

"Indeed, I did!"

"I don't understand. Why didn't a super-nice Mr. Masters come back to our room? Why did he just leave?" I jumped up from my chair. "I know. I'll bet he was so used to being mean that he couldn't stand the idea of being nice to everyone!"

"Allan! Are you going to let me tell the story, or are you just going to continue to interrupt?"

"Sorry," I said.

Mrs. Mullins took another long sip of tea. "All right. As I was saying, I scattered the magic powder on him, and I was just about to finish saying the word *nice*, when some child in the room we were standing next to yelled *fish*. Well, that was the first word that he heard, and you know what the spell says. . . ." She spread her hands out and shrugged.

"You mean . . . oh wow . . . I don't . . . I mean . . ." I stopped for a minute. "Mr. Masters *didn't* leave, did he?"

Mrs. Mullins shook her head no.

I jumped off the sofa. "Oh my gosh. He's the fish swimming in the bathtub in our classroom, right?"

"Absolutely correct," Mrs. Mullins replied.

I didn't know quite what to say, and then it just sort of popped out. "No wonder he's such a big, ugly fish!" Little bits began to dawn on me. "And that's why you knew for sure that we'd need a sub for tomorrow. You knew Mr. Masters couldn't possibly come back to teach the class because he wasn't ever gone. He was just swimming round and round in that big old bathtub." I began to laugh. "Boy, if I'd known it was Mr. Masters, I wouldn't have worked so hard to keep the fish alive."

Mrs. Mullins tapped her sneaker on the floor. "Nonsense. Since it was Mr. Masters it was even more important to keep the fish alive. That's the only way he can return to being a person."

"Wow." I took my Cubs hat off, and put it on again backward, which helped me think. I didn't like Mr. Masters, but I didn't want to be part of killing a person. I looked at Mrs. Mullins, and I could tell that she was really worried. I reached out and patted her arm. "Don't worry, Mrs. Mullins, I'll make sure that the sub keeps an eye on that fish tomorrow."

She sighed even more deeply. She took her granny glasses off and laid them on the table. Her voice was so soft and so low that I barely heard it. "Allan, tomorrow I am the sub."

10

"You?" I gasped. "But Mrs. Mullins, you . . . I mean, I don't . . . I mean why?"

Mrs. Mullins took another sip of her tea. "I don't want to be your substitute, that's for certain. But Principal Dugan didn't leave me a great deal of choice. He asked me numerous times what exactly I had said to Mr. Masters. He seemed so perplexed that Mr. Masters would just suddenly leave. Then he said he just didn't know where he could get a substitute for your class. It was hard enough even with notice because of your class's reputation. Then he looked at me, and said that it seemed as if I got along with all of you."

"Why didn't you tell him no, that you've got to stuff to do?"

"I did, but he persisted. He smiled at me, a very you-will-do-this kind of smile," she explained. And I knew just what she meant. I'd seen that principalish smile myself a few times.

It was sort of a smile, but it didn't mean he was happy. Once, when I'd seen two kids fighting on the playground, Mr. Dugan called me into his office. He smiled at me and then smiled some more when he said, "Now, Allan, I know you'll want to tell me all about what was going on this morning." It was definitely a command. I nodded, "Yes, Mrs. Mullins, I think I understand."

"Besides, Mr. Dugan kept repeating how strange he thought it was for Mr. Masters to have just disappeared." She tried to make her scratchy voice sound real low. "He said, 'You know, Mrs. Mullins, in all my years as a principal I've never had a substitute just take off. And Mr. Masters seemed like a man so fully in control of the situation.' "

Mrs. Mullins put her glasses back on and stared at me. "Allan, Mr. Dugan shook his head, and said that it was almost like some sort of strange magic that a man like Mr. Masters could just *poof* disappear without a word. Well, when he said that, I couldn't take the chance. I didn't want Principal Dugan to keep investigating, and it seemed that the only way to get him to drop the whole thing was to agree to be your substitute. So . . . what do I have to do to be a teacher?"

I stuck my hands in my pocket. I had never really thought about what a teacher had to do. It seemed to me that it had to be a whole lot easier than being a student. For one thing, you already knew all the answers to all the tests! But being a substitute teacher for our fifth-grade class was a whole other story. Of course, maybe after Mr. Masters, the kids would be so glad to have someone nice that they wouldn't give Mrs. Mullins such a hard time.

"Earth to Allan," Mrs. Mullins said. "I need your help."

"Right," I said. "Well, I guess you just follow Mrs. Evans's lesson plans."

She looked at me. "I thought you said that Mr. Masters threw them away the first day."

"Yeah, I guess he did." I tried to think. "Well, first, we usually have spelling."

Mrs. Mullins held up her hand. "Just a minute, let me get some paper." She went over to a drawer under the cabinet and pulled out a pad of paper. She came back to the table. "Okay, I'm ready to take notes."

I looked at the paper. "Uh . . . I don't think you'd better use that!"

Mrs. Mullins's face got red. The paper had stuff on the top that said U.S. Witches' Association. "Oh, my!" she exclaimed. "What could I have been thinking!" She rushed back to get different paper, and while she got it, I played hide-and-seek with my conscience. I mean a grown-up was asking me what our class should have to do. My answer . . . I wanted to say only fun stuff or nothing. But Mrs. Mullins was my friend, and was only in this whole mess because of me. If we didn't do school-type stuff in class tomorrow, Mr. Dugan would probably be in asking lots more questions.

In the end, being a good friend seemed a little better than not having to do any work tomorrow, and Mrs. Mullins and I sat down and tried to plan a day. I did remind her that if we worked hard in the morning, we'd need the afternoon to begin on our fish project. Mrs. Mullins took lots of notes, and when she finally put everything aside, she said her hand hurt. I told her that I knew just what she meant. Mr. Monster-Sub had practically worn ours out.

Mrs. Mullins stood up from the kitchen table and clapped her hands together. "Now, that we've got this whole thing sort of under control, will you help me with my dress? I want to get it made in time to buy shoes to match it."

I looked at her feet. "Okay, I'll help, but why can't you just wear your sneakers? I wear mine everywhere."

Mrs. Mullins chuckled. "Just take my word for it. Sneakers would not do for a tea."

I stood next to her as she started to make up her mixture. She didn't get the recipe book out. I guessed that since this was the third time she was making the potion for a new tea dress, she must know the recipe by heart. As she combined things, she said, "I decided that I'll make my dress green. I've had quite enough of pink, I think!" She hummed as she put together ingredients. This was clearly a witch who loved her work. As she took down a jar, she said, "You know, I almost forgot. I have this powder I've never tried, but it's supposed to hurry things up. I think I'll dump some of it in so we can get this dress done before anything else gets in the way." She took out a big measuring spoon and poured some of the jar's powder into the spoon. Then she stirred the new powder into the rest of her ingredients. In just seconds, the mixture started to turn green. Mrs. Mullins stood over it, "Oh, I think I'm really going to like this! It's actually a much nicer color than the pink, don't you think?"

I really didn't think much about the color one way or the other. Mrs. Mullins continued, "Hmm, I thought it might be a forest green, but it looks more like the color an elf would wear! How charming." She began to chant:

"The green of an elf I want to wear.
The green of an elf I want to be there."

She looked at me. "Okay," she whispered, "now, pour the potion over me."

"Are you sure?" I whispered back, still thinking of what happened to the pink. I wasn't quite sure why I was whispering since we were the only two people in the house, but somehow, it seemed like a good idea.

She motioned for me to pour. I did. The green slid down Mrs. Mullins, but it didn't stay on her, and thank goodness it didn't leave her skin green at all. But it was weird stuff. When it hit the ground, it didn't spread out like stuff usually does when you spill it, it formed into this glowing little ball. It got real bright. Mrs. Mullins clapped her hands twice. "Now, watch," she said excitedly, "my dress should appear."

Still the small ball of green glowed. Mrs. Mullins looked a little perplexed. "Hmm," she said almost to herself. She clapped again. "Appear, now!" she commanded.

"Oh, hold your horses," came a very tiny voice.

"Allan, are you playing games?" She looked at me sternly.

"I like games a lot," the tiny voice said again. "I want to play, too."

"That's not me," I whispered, staring at the green ball.

The tiny voice said, "What's not me? What kind of a game is 'That's Not Me'?"

The green ball began to dissolve, and first, I saw a little green-booted foot appear. I rubbed my eyes hard because I knew I couldn't be seeing what I thought I was seeing. When I took my hands away from my eyes, there wasn't anything on the floor. I shook my head. I felt sort of stupid. I decided I wouldn't say anything to Mrs. Mullins. My eyes must have been playing tricks on me. I'd just ask about Mrs. Mullins's dress. "So . . ." I started to say.

"So what?!" came that high-pitched voice. I turned to see where it was coming from, and there was an elf standing on Mrs. Mullins's sewing machine. It had on a bright green hat with a feather on the top, bright green shirt and tights, and of course, the little green boots that I'd seen but thought I must be imagining. Maybe I was still imagining now. I wanted to ask Mrs. Mullins if she saw anything, but my mouth just sort of stayed open and no sound came out.

The little green elf took his hat off, bowed low, and swept it back up onto his head. "Himself the elf!" he announced.

"I've come to play.
I don't have all day.
You've got my name.
What's the game?"

Mrs. Mullins and I stared at the elf and then at each other. Himself the elf, shook his tiny little head. He was no bigger than my hand. He jumped off the sewing machine onto my shoulder. It was pretty weird; I'd once had a bird on my shoulder, but never a little person.

Mrs. Mullins peered at Himself. "I'm terribly

sorry, but there is no game here. I was just trying to make a dress. I'm afraid that you'll just have to go back to wherever you came from because we don't have time for any games with elves today. We were only trying to make a new dress. I am very sorry for your inconvenience; it won't happen again." She said it very firmly. For a minute, it popped into my head that she just might be okay as a substitute teacher.

Himself stomped his foot. "Hey, that's my shoulder you're stomping on," I said, still not really letting myself believe that I was talking to an elf.

> "You're no fun, the two of you!
> So I'll do what I want to do."

With that Himself the elf jumped off my shoulder back onto the sewing machine. Mrs. Mullins had the window open behind the sewing machine, and the next thing we knew Himself jumped right out the window.

"Oh dear! Oh no! We just can't have an elf darting about the backyard. What if people see him?" Mrs. Mullins was almost wringing her hands. "Come on, Allan; we've got to find him. If you can get him back in here, I'll start looking for a recipe to make him disappear. We've got to hurry. What if Blanche Switzer looks over the fence and sees him?"

I didn't even want to think about what that old busybody would spread around the neighborhood if she saw an elf in Mrs. Mullins's backyard. I went out the back door. I wasn't quite sure how I'd get him back inside. Besides, Mrs. Mullins's backyard was so green with lawn and trees that it was hard to even spot him. "Uh, hey, Himself," I called.

There was no response. "Hey, come on. I really would like to play a game with you. Come on up on the picnic table, and we'll talk." In an instant the little green figure was standing on the picnic table. I thought about just reaching out and grabbing him, but I was afraid that if he got away, I'd never get hold of him again. Himself was standing with his tiny little hands on his hips. His whole hands were no bigger than the tip of my fingernail. I leaned toward him. "Why don't you just come inside and we'll play a game."

His little blue eyes glared at me.

"Oh yeah? You'd better make it something good. Or I'm off to see your neighborhood."

"Well . . ." I tried to think. I didn't know what kind of game would appeal to an elf. Until five minutes ago, I'd thought elves were only made-up creatures. I guessed it didn't really matter what I said; I just had to get him inside so Mrs.

Mullins could make him disappear back to wherever he belonged. "Well," I said again, "there are lots of games inside. You can choose."

Himself jumped off the table and I could hear his high-pitched voice call from the grass, "How about this:

> I will hide, and you can seek.
> 'Cuz I don't play well with a geek."

That does it! I thought. *I've had enough. I'm going inside. I'm going home. No normal ten-year-old kid spends his afternoons talking with imaginary elves.* I started toward the house. *A geek,* I thought. *Things couldn't get much worse than some puny-sized, imaginary person calling me a geek.*

As I reached the door, I heard Mrs. Mullins's voice. "Oh, Allan! I think I've found just the recipe. I'll start to get it ready. Thank you for finding our little guest. You are some super friend."

I took my hand back off the doorknob. Guilt. If the elf really took off, he was bound to cause trouble. An imaginary elf popping up all over would soon be the talk of the town, and with Mr. Masters swimming around as a fish, it wouldn't be too long before busybody Blanche Switzer began to find reasons for such strange happenings.

I couldn't let Mrs. Mullins down. I had to think of something to get that dumb elf out of the lawn and into my hand. First, I had to find him — again.

"Himself?" I called.

There was silence. *Great,* I thought. *Who knew if the elf was even still in the lawn?* Then I had an idea. "Fine. Don't answer." I called out. "I know you're there. You think you can jump so high, but you're nothing so great. I could jump higher than you any old day."

With that I heard a tiny,

"Ha! That's a dumb game, and this place is a
    bore.
So I'm outta here. I'll try next door."

Then I saw Himself make a mighty leap and land right in Miss Switzer's backyard. He couldn't have picked a worse spot.

I ran to the redwood fence that stretched between Mrs. Mullins's and Miss Switzer's backyards, and I hoisted myself up enough to see over the top. "Himself," I called trying to imitate that mother/teacher voice that made you freeze right where you were and do whatever the voice commanded. "You come back here immediately!"

Himself giggled a really high-pitched awful laugh.

"No and, a big ha-ha on you.
There are tricks I want to do.
You just watch and you can see.
I am where I want to be!"

Then I saw Himself leap up right through the open window of Miss Switzer's house. For a minute, I just stood there, unwilling to believe what had happened. I didn't even want to think about what that mean munchkin was doing to Miss Switzer's. I trudged back to Mrs. Mullins's house. What could I tell her? That not only had I not gotten hold of the green menace, but at this very moment, he was probably making a complete mess in the house of the biggest gossip in town?

11

I opened the back screen door to Mrs. Mullins's house. "Oh, Allan, is that you?"

"Uh-huh," I kind of muttered.

"How nice!" Mrs. Mullins sounded relieved and excited. "Why don't you just invite our little guest into the kitchen, and we'll all have a wonderful snack? He's probably hungry and ready to go home."

"I don't think so," I mumbled to myself. I took a deep breath and walked into the kitchen. There was no point to dragging this out. "Himself isn't with me," I said feeling sorry for myself and Mrs. Mullins.

Mrs. Mullins looked at me. "Was . . . was he just wanting to stay outside?" She didn't wait for an answer, maybe because she didn't want to hear the answer I was going to give. She clapped her hands quickly. "You know we could always take this potion out there. I found the most perfect return-from-where-you-started recipe in my magic book, and it wasn't even hard to make, so let's go out to Himself and get him home immediately. I'll bet his mother already misses him."

"I'll bet he doesn't even have a mother," I mumbled.

"Pardon me?" Mrs. Mullins said.

I couldn't make myself look at her. I didn't want to see the expression on Mrs. Mullins's face when I told her what I had to say. I stared at the floor wishing I could sink into it, as I said, "We can't just go get him outside because he's not there. He's at Miss Switzer's. He went in through an open window."

Mrs. Mullins's hand flew to her face, and she looked truly shocked. "Oh, my word! I never . . . I mean of all the places . . . oh dear." She sank down into a kitchen chair, and took off her glasses. Her eyes were filled with tears. "Well, I guess I might as well start packing."

I felt terrible. "Hey, it'll be okay, Mrs. Mullins. Really it will. I mean your spells always wear off. He'll just get back home on his own sooner or later."

Mrs. Mullins put her glasses on again and stared at me. "But we both know that we can't wait for sooner or later. Blanche Switzer is sure that there's a witch in this town somewhere. All she needs is a little green elf hopping through her house telling her that *I* was the one who made him appear."

She was right, of course. We had to get that little troublemaker gone and fast. "How about if we just go into Miss Switzer's and find him?" I asked.

"Hmm, I guess it would be possible. I'll take some of this potion powder with us, and we'll have to hope we find him before she does. I'll start talking with her about the tea, and you . . ." she ran her hand through her hair to think.

"And I'll say that I need to use the bathroom, and once I'm out of her living room, I'll find Himself and sneak him back to you. Then you can dump a little of your magic on him, and *poof*, he'll be history."

"Good," said Mrs. Mullins. "Then at least we have a plan."

The truth was that it wasn't much of a plan. Miss Switzer hated having kids in her house. She acted as if she liked us when other grown-ups were around, but I knew that the only reason she talked to kids at all was to try to find out secrets we knew. She was so yucky that we even skipped her house on Halloween. I didn't really think she was going to be very thrilled about my visit even with Mrs. Mullins, and she certainly was not going to let me wander through her house by myself. But, I didn't have any other plan, so I watched Mrs. Mullins put a little of the potion she had made in her handkerchief, and we headed next door to disaster.

Mrs. Mullins took a book with her about drying flowers. She figured that if she had something to give Miss Switzer that might keep Miss Switzer from getting distracted by anything like, say, a little green elf. We rang the doorbell, and my heart was pumping real hard. I wondered if Mrs. Mullins could possibly be as nervous as I was, and then I saw how tightly she was grasping the book. Her fingers had turned white.

Blanche Switzer looked through the peephole and then called, "Is that you, Henrietta?"

"Yes, Blanche," Mrs. Mullins said. "I . . . uh . . . wanted to show you something I learned in this book about drying flowers."

"Well, just a minute." We heard the sound of a dead bolt being turned and a chain being taken off the door. Miss Switzer opened the door for Mrs. Mullins and started to shut it again.

"Uh, hi," I said, following Mrs. Mullins in the house.

"Well, Henrietta, you certainly are full of surprises. Why on earth did you bring the boy with you?" she asked as if I didn't have ears and couldn't hear.

Mrs. Mullins turned toward me. "Oh, Allan, well he's very interested in flowers, aren't you, Allan?"

"Oh, yes," I lied. "I love drying flowers."

Miss Switzer ignored me. "So, Henrietta, how do you like my new security system? As president of the Block Watch, I felt I ought to set an example. What about this dead bolt? And I have an alarm! And you wouldn't believe what I found out about houses without alarm systems. You really should contact the company and have one installed. I'll tell you; it feels good for me to know that there is no way anyone could ever be in my house without my knowing all about it!"

She looked so impressed with herself that I felt like saying, "Wanna bet? There's a tiny green brat probably taking apart the back of your house right this very second, and you have no idea it's happening." Of course, I didn't say anything at all.

"Well, I'll have to look into an alarm."

"No, don't look into it! Do it." Miss Switzer shook her dyed yellow hair to emphasize her point. "I tell you there is something strange that's going on in this town, and until I get to the bottom of it, an alarm is important. I checked, and my sister-in-law's sister's mother said she was sure she heard something about a witch moving here. Boy, that witch better never tangle with Blanche Switzer!"

Mrs. Mullins was turning paler by the moment. I wondered if Miss Switzer noticed how shaky Mrs. Mullins sounded when she said, "Blanche, I really want you to see this book. Allan, ask Miss Switzer if you can go wash your hands before you touch my special book."

That was supposed to be my cue to locate Himself the elf while Mrs. Mullins kept Miss Switzer busy. It wasn't much of a plan, but we didn't exactly have a whole lot of time to figure it out.

I started to get up, and then I stopped. A bright green munchkin had popped up on Miss Switzer's coffee table. We were doomed.

There was only one thing we could do. Nothing. I was holding my breath. I didn't know if it would be better to try to grab Himself and get him out of there, or if I'd only create even more of a scene. Either way, I felt pretty sure that our secret was about to explode. I tried to catch Mrs. Mullins's eye to find out how we should react, but she was looking at Miss Switzer.

"You?!" Miss Switzer said in an amazed and accusing voice. "What are you? How did you get here? What are you doing?"

What Himself was doing was standing on top of the candy, bending over the candy dish and taking a bite of each of the chocolates on it.

"Henrietta," Miss Switzer whispered. "Do you see what I see?"

I took a deep breath. What could Mrs. Mullins possibly say.

She looked at Miss Switzer, and she said, "You mean the new chocolates you've put out? They look delicious." I couldn't believe it. Mrs. Mullins was terrific. How could she say that with a straight face!

Miss Switzer was irritated. "No, not the chocolates, look . . . look at the little green . . . green . . . pixie taking bites out of each piece of candy. You must see him. I know those little things are only in stories, they're not real, but there he is."

Mrs. Mullins didn't say a word.

Miss Switzer had two bright red spots on her cheeks. "Henrietta, you must get your glasses checked immediately! You, Allan, you see this little thing, don't you?"

Himself was oblivious to our conversation. He had climbed into the candy dish, pushed one chocolate-covered cherry from the dish onto the table, and he looked as if he were preparing to jump from the top of the candy dish right into the middle of the candy.

I looked right back at Miss Switzer. "Uh, gee, it looks like a piece of candy fell off the dish, is that what you mean?"

"What's wrong with the two of you?" Miss Switzer demanded. "There, that elf just jumped into the chocolate. He's standing in it up to his knees. Surely, you must see it."

Mrs. Mullins's eyes began to twinkle just a little. "Gee, Blanche, I don't know. Maybe you have some sort of magical powers or something that ordinary people like Allan and me don't have."

I bit the inside of my cheek to keep from laughing. "Yeah, wow, are you — can you do magic?" I asked her.

"Well, how dare you! I've never been so insulted. Everyone knows that I can't stand witches or magic or any of that sort of thing. Someone is going to pay for this!" Miss Switzer looked thoroughly upset. We had her on the run now.

Then Himself spoke.

"This chocolate stuff is really neat.
And now I think I'll have a seat."

And with that, Himself sat down right in the middle of the cherry.

Miss Switzer gasped. "And it talks, too. You heard it, didn't you? You had to have heard it. I'm going to put out an all-points bulletin for my Block Watch group!"

Himself uttered a big burp for such a little elf, and then he leaped from the chocolate-covered cherry right onto the front of Miss Switzer's dress. His feet and legs were covered with cherry goo, and when he landed on Miss Switzer's dress, it made a big red splat. Between the green elf and the red spot, she looked a little like Christmas. But I don't think Miss Switzer had her mind on Christmas. In fact, she took one look at her dress and the elf, gave a little soft scream, and then she fainted.

Himself was still sitting on Miss Switzer wondering why he was now on the floor. I guess elves didn't know much about fainting. Mrs. Mullins leapt up from her chair and rushed toward Himself. She moved really fast for an old lady. Before Himself moved again, she dumped the contents of her handkerchief on him. He looked up to see falling white powder begin to cover him. "Hey . . ."

"You must return home," Mrs. Mullins said, as she finished sprinkling her magic powder.

"No, I won't, and you can't . . ." the elf's tiny voice began to fade, and in an instant he had disappeared. Mrs. Mullins and I looked at each other and then back at Miss Switzer.

"Wow," I said. "Pretty amazing. You did it. He's gone! Boy, we sure came close to getting caught that time!"

"Too close," Mrs. Mullins said.

Miss Switzer was starting to come to. "Whaa . . . what happened?"

Mrs. Mullins looked at me, took a deep breath, and then turned her attention to Miss Switzer. "Why Blanche, you fainted. We were quite concerned. Are you feeling better? Maybe you've got a fever."

"But . . . I saw . . ." Miss Switzer started to look around the room.

All of a sudden, I realized that Himself's pointed green hat was still on the floor right next to Miss Switzer's arm. It must have fallen from his head when she'd fainted. Green proof that Miss Switzer hadn't imagined all this. My heart was pounding. I could feel it thump in my chest as I tried to casually walk over, bend down, and scoop the hat into my pocket. My fingers touched the felt. Victory! Even Mrs. Mullins didn't notice what I was doing. She was standing over Miss Switzer playing the properly concerned friend.

She patted Miss Switzer gently on the arm. "Here, let me help you up." She took Miss Switzer's arm and got her into the chair from which she'd fallen. "You know, Blanche," Mrs. Mullins said soothingly, "you work so hard keeping this neighborhood safe for all of us. Perhaps, you've been under too much stress."

For once, Miss Switzer looked a little perplexed. For once, she was not in charge. "Yes, I do work very hard. I believe I'll take a little rest, and then I'll think about . . . about all of this . . . this later!"

"We'll just let ourselves out," Mrs. Mullins said softly. She caught my eye and motioned toward the door. In a minute we were in the front yard. "We're awesome!" I said grinning. "I think we really confused that old busybody! Maybe she'll leave you alone now, huh? After all, it wasn't us who saw imaginary elves, huh?"

Mrs. Mullins took her glasses off and rubbed

her eyes. "I hope you're right. I'm just getting too old for this sort of thing!"

"Oh, you're not old, Mrs. Mullins. I mean look how fast you got to Himself with that powder. I mean you were there before he could even move. But you know, I was wondering, exactly where did Himself go?"

"Home," she said firmly, "which is something we should do, too. And please — no more questions today." I reached deep into my pocket and felt the little piece of material there. I didn't think that now would be a good time to show Mrs. Mullins that I still had the elf's hat, but I was glad I had it.

12

Mrs. Mullins went to her house, and I went home to mine. When I got there, my mom was home from work and the smell of dinner was coming from the kitchen. "How was your day, honey?" she asked.

"Uhh, fine," I said. I let my fingers curl around Himself's hat, but I didn't say anything to my mom. Somehow, I thought that all I would get was grounded if I told her that I'd spent the afternoon with an obnoxious little green elf who was about the size of her finger. "My day was just fine."

"Oh, good, then Mr. Masters wasn't so bad today." She put a big bowl of macaroni and cheese on the table, and I sat down to eat. "See, I told you things would work out. Sometimes, substitutes just have to feel like they have a firm hand on things, and then they let up."

I had almost forgotten about Mr. Masters! "Well, Mom, I'm not sure how much of a hand he has on things!" I said, biting my lip to keep from laughing as I thought to myself, a fin maybe, but definitely not a hand. I wondered how he was doing swimming around in his bathtub and probably being hungry. It served him right for being so mean to us kids; it would be good for him to feel a little unhappy after the way he'd tortured us all week. Still, I figured that Mrs. Mullins was right. I didn't want to kill him or anything, so I guessed we'd need to get him some food. "Mom," I said taking a big mouthful of macaroni in my mouth, "what do piranhas eat?"

"What?" my mother asked. "I can't understand you when you talk with your mouth full!"

I swallowed my macaroni. It was especially cheesy tonight. Maybe asking what a piranha ate wasn't the best way to tell my mom about the fish we'd gotten, so I just said, "Mom, this is the best dinner!"

She beamed. "Why thank you, Allan. I know it's your favorite dinner, and I figured that since you've been having kind of a rough week that you could use the treat. I just wish I could be here more for you, but at least we've got Mrs. Mullins to help us out."

My mom worked really hard. Ever since she and my dad had split up, she seemed to be really busy with her job. "Yeah," I said, trying to decide how to break the news about the piranha before someone else mentioned that I was the one who'd brought it in. "Actually, we thought up a great plan for my class project, and she even helped me get it."

"Oh?" my mother said.

So I told her that Mrs. Mullins had brought a fish to school for me this morning, and that our class was going to study it, write reports about it, and actually show it during the school's science fair.

"That sounds wonderful," she smiled. "What kind of fish?"

"A piranha."

Mom's brown eyes got big. "A piranha? Allan, aren't those dangerous? Wherever did she get a piranha? They don't even sell them in pet stores."

I looked at her. Why was it that moms always asked good questions that you really couldn't answer if you wanted to tell the truth, and then they looked right through you while they waited for an answer. I began to wish I had never said anything to her in the first place, but then how would I have ever explained it when she just walked into the school's science fair and saw the huge fish.

"Oh, Mrs. Mullins and I found it." I didn't really want to say more, so I got up from my chair. "You know, Mom, you look kind of tired. How about if I clear the table and do the dishes!"

"Allan." She stood and hugged me. "You are one terrific son!"

"Not really," I answered feeling kind of guilty. I cleared the table and did the dishes. I didn't even mind sticking them in the dishwasher because I had a lot to think about. Tomorrow was going to be quite a day with Mrs. Mullins as our substitute teacher and Mr. Monster-Sub swimming around in a bathtub as a piranha.

13

When I got to school the next morning, Mrs. Mullins was already there. I had been going to wish her good luck about subbing, but there were some other kids already in there in the front of the room, so I just caught her eye and nodded. As more kids came into the room, the group around the bathtub grew and grew.

"Boy," Amanda said, "that sure is one ugly fish. I told my mom about it last night. She didn't even want to believe me at first. She said there was no way we could have a real live piranha."

"Yeah," Justin said, "it's alive all right. Look at those teeth! Boy I'd like to stick that old Mr. Monster-Sub's fingers in that fish's mouth. Chomp, chomp!"

"Ugh!" Candice said, "that's disgusting."

Andy slugged Justin in the arm. "Ugh!" In a high girlish voice, he mimicked, "Oh Justin, you're just disgusting!"

People laughed, and Candice said, "Very funny."

"Thanks, I thought so," Andy said.

Meanwhile, the bell had rung, and everyone was still standing around the bathtub. "Uh, maybe you should sit down now," Mrs. Mullins said softly. No one paid any attention.

"All right, students. It's time to get started."

No one moved. A voice from the back of the crowd around the bathtub said, "Hey, you guys up in front, you already had a turn up close. Move back and let us see better." Other kids in the back shouted in agreement. People started sort of pushing each other. Mrs. Mullins looked at me, and I could see the pleading in her eyes.

I tried to think fast. I couldn't look like some goody-goody, but I couldn't leave my friend Mrs. Mullins to get off on such a bad start. I didn't know what to do, and then suddenly, I had an idea. I shouted, "Uh . . . you guys. I think I hear the principal coming down the hall. Quick. Hit your seats!"

There was mass confusion as everyone dove for their seat and rummaged to get their paper and pencils so we could look as if we were working by the time Principal Dugan got there. Mrs. Mullins shot me a look of thanks.

"I don't hear anything," Andy said.

Mrs. Mullins walked toward the door, opened it, peeked out, and waved. "Yes indeed, Mr.

Dugan, we're off to a fine start," she said.

I tried not to smile. Mrs. Mullins and I made a pretty good pair. I covered for her. She covered for me. She walked back to the front of the class. "All right," she said, "now that I have your attention, I've been thinking about what we should do for today and tomorrow."

Justin raised his hand, and without waiting to be called on said, "Nothing! How about doing nothing!"

Mrs. Mullins walked over to his desk. Her red sneakers squeaked on the floor as she walked. Everyone waited to see what would happen. But Mrs. Mullins didn't say anything to him; she just stood right in front of his desk and continued, "If we work really hard in the mornings, we can spend the afternoons getting our information and display ready for the school's science fair. If not . . . well, I don't know when we can do the preparation for the fair if you know what I mean."

She walked back to her desk. "Now, let's start with spelling." Everyone groaned, but the spelling assignment wasn't too bad. In fact, after Mr. Masters, this assignment seemed like a piece of cake. It was great to get recess back, too. All in all, the morning went pretty fast, and then it was lunchtime!

While I was eating, I heard Justin say something to Andy, and Andy whispered something to

Jennifer, but I didn't know what it was. Jennifer giggled.

When we got back from lunch, we walked into the classroom. We went to our seats, and Mrs. Mullins went to her desk. "Oh, oh, dear," she said. Her hand flew to her mouth.

Everyone craned their heads to see what possibly could be wrong. It looked as if someone had gotten sick all over Mrs. Mullins's desk. She went over to the paper towel dispenser and got some towels to clean it up, but when she went to wipe it, the whole thing lifted up. Fake vomit. Everyone laughed and wondered just what our new substitute would do about this.

They didn't have to wait long. She scooped it up and held the thing between her two fingers. "I believe someone has lost this. Would anyone like to claim it?"

There was silence for a minute. Then Justin said, "Oh my gosh. I can't believe it. Someone must have stolen it from inside my desk. Gosh I'm so sorry." He grinned.

Mrs. Mullins looked at him and tapped her foot. Her eyes were glowing with anger. The fake vomit was still right between her fingers. "You know, when I was in school there was a saying, 'Finders keepers.' " She dropped the thing inside the teacher's drawer in her desk. Justin glared at her, but Mrs. Mullins didn't seem to notice.

She walked to the board and picked up a piece of chalk. "What do you think we should do to get ready for this school's science fair?"

Jennifer raised her hand. "First of all, I think we should name our fish. I want to call him Mr. P. It's short for piranha, but it makes him seem like he's like real." Everyone voted, and we agreed to call him Mr. P.

Amanda said, "Don't you think that Mr. P must be hungry? I mean we just had lunch and stuff, and he hasn't had anything to eat at all."

Everyone looked at me. "Uhh, well . . . I . . . uh, well, I know they like to eat live stuff. I'll go back to the pet store after school."

Andy raised his hand. "I've got some worms in my desk."

Mrs. Mullins pushed the glasses up on her nose. "You've got what in your desk?"

Andy got a little red. "Well, uh, I was gonna use 'em for something." Justin grinned, and I had a pretty good idea that they had brought them to play a trick on Mrs. Mullins. Better they should feed them to Mr. P.

Jennifer asked, "Do piranhas like worms?"

"Uh, uh," Andy said. "Maybe it's like my mother and spinach. She says, 'If you're hungry enough . . .' "

Andy picked up a squirmy, fat worm and pulled it out of a paper cup of dirt. The whole class followed him to the bathtub and there was a big OH as he dropped it in. The worm wiggled its way to the bottom, and the fish swam around it. Mr. P did not seem interested in eating it at all. I promised myself that I would go to the pet store today. Meanwhile, I hoped that Andy was right and a worm was no worse for Mr. P than spinach was for us.

Mrs. Mullins sent us back to our seats. "You'll never get finished if you spend all your time watching the piranha. Fish don't have to eat every single day. We'll make sure we have the right food for Mr. P tomorrow." So we divided into groups to work on all different parts of our report on piranhas. We got to sit on the floor to work on posters, and we could talk while we worked. It was actually fun, and by the end of the day, it looked like we might really have a chance at pulling off a pretty great project. As we were waiting for the final bell, Candice raised her hand. "I heard that Mrs. Johnson's sixth grade is doing a report on bees, but all they have is a hive and some pictures. I think we're the only ones with a terrible-looking live animal, so we ought to say thanks to Allan." She smiled at me, and Jeff leaned over and gave me a high five.

After school, I told Mrs. Mullins I'd go to the pet store, and I left, feeling pretty darn good about things. Mrs. Mullins had been a decent substitute, and except for the fake vomit, no one had even given her a hard time. That in itself was pretty amazing.

I headed for the pet store, and as I walked I thought, *The school's science fair is on-track; Mr. Monster-Sub is safely stored away. We're just one day away from victory.*

When I got into the pet store, I found a guy in a blue jacket with a name tag that said ASK ME.

"I need to buy some piranha food," I said.

His eyes got big. "Piranha food? Whoa. Pet stores can't even sell piranhas."

"Right, but I'm not trying to buy one. I just need some food for one. Do you sell food they can eat?"

He called over another blue jacket, and pretty soon, I had about four of them staring at me. "Kid, what are you doing with a piranha? They can be dangerous," one said.

I sighed. I had a feeling that I didn't really want to get into all this, so I answered, "I didn't say I had a piranha. I just wanted to know what they ate."

The blue jackets began to drift away. I was no longer very interesting. One guy said over his shoulder, "I guess live goldfish would do it. We've got some books over there that you can look at. Maybe they could tell you more."

I glanced at a book. It wasn't much help. I

found another salesman, picked out six feeder goldfish, watched the salesman scoop them into a net and tie them into a plastic bag filled with water. Tomorrow Mr. P would have food.

As I headed home, I thought of Mrs. Mullins. Her tea party was Saturday. If she helped us all day tomorrow and then went to the school's science fair, she wouldn't have any time to make her dress. I decided to stop by her house, show her my goldfish, and see if she wanted me to help her make magic.

When I got there, I knocked on the door. "Is that you, Allan?" came a voice from inside.

"Uh-huh," I answered.

"Well, the door is open. I'm too pooped to get up and answer it. Come on in." I walked into Mrs. Mullins's living room, and she was stretched out on the sofa, her red sneakers hanging over one end. "Gee, this teaching is tiring stuff. I'm glad tomorrow is my last day."

I smiled. "Yeah, this learning stuff is pretty tiring, too, and I have to do it forever." I stuck out my goldfish bag. "Look — lunch for Mr. P."

"Good," she said, "we wouldn't want Mr. Masters to get too hungry."

I shrugged. "You know, it was pretty neat the way Candice thanked me for getting Mr. P. I mean she did it in front of the whole class."

Mrs. Mullins smiled at me. "She's a cute little girl."

I could feel my face getting red. "Anyway, I came by to see if I could help you with some magic for your dress."

Mrs. Mullins sighed. "I just don't know what I'll do about that. I have nothing I can wear, but today I'm just too tired to try any other spells."

I looked at the blue dress Mrs. Mullins was wearing. It seemed okay to me. I didn't know why she couldn't just wear it, but I guessed it was something like having the right baseball hat. I mean I had to have my Cubs hat to bring me luck.

I walked over and sat down in the chair facing the sofa. "Mrs. Mullins, with the fair and everything, I don't think we'll have time to make you your dress tomorrow. Why don't you try another quick spell now. This time I'm sure you'll get it right." There was a part of me that really did want her to have that new dress, and another part of me that really wanted to see another magical spell. But the reason didn't matter because the magic just wasn't to be. The phone rang, and Mrs. Mullins got up to answer it. It was my mom. She'd gotten off work early, and she wanted Mrs. Mullins to send me home right away.

As I left, Mrs. Mullins sank back down in the sofa. I hoped she was going to be okay. "See you tomorrow?"

"Why don't you come to school early and help

me make sure I've got everything ready." She smiled. "After all, tomorrow's the day the fifth grade wins the school's science fair, and I retire from teaching!"

As soon as I got home, my mom asked me all about the fair. She said one of the ladies at work had a fourth-grader at our school, and he said that our class was the one to beat. She said that his mom had gone on and on. I didn't say too much. I didn't want to jinx our victory so I just told Mom that she could see everything when she came the next night.

"Allan, I wouldn't miss it for the world!" Mom promised.

When I went to bed, I knew I should have been feeling really happy. I mean Mrs. Mullins was a good sub. We were rid of Mr. Masters and we had a great school fair project for which Candice had thanked *me* in front of everyone. I was sure we were going to win first place with it, and then maybe, Candice would tell the whole class how great I was. It all sounded terrific. Yet somehow, I didn't feel very happy. Somehow, I had this strange feeling that something just wasn't quite right.

I fell asleep for a little bit and dreamed that when I got to school the next day, the bathtub, the piranha, and everything we'd made for the fair was gone. All the kids were mad at me, and Jennifer Swanson tossed her head, glared at me, and said, "Allan Hobart messed everything up again!"

"But . . . but I didn't!" Everyone started yelling at me. They wouldn't listen. "Really, I didn't!"

I was really relieved to wake up and find out I was having a nightmare. But, once I was awake, I tossed and turned all night. I made myself think about good things like our class winning the school's science fair and what it would be like to have everyone congratulating me for my good idea. But I couldn't shake this awful feeling . . .

When it was time to get up, I was glad. I got dressed fast, grabbed a Pop-Tart and some milk, and called to my mom that I was going to school early to work on the fair. She came in the kitchen. "My goodness, you *are* ready early." She was still wearing her robe. "After school, come home for dinner, and we'll go back together. In fact, why don't you invite Mrs. Mullins? She's been so nice."

"Uhh, I don't know. If we don't get finished, we may have to stay at school. Could I call your office, and if I have to stay, would you bring me a Big Mac and a double order of fries for Mrs. Mullins, too?"

My mom ruffled my hair. "Okay, hon. You've got it. Call me and give me your order. In fact if you want the Big Mac, we can have it even if you come home."

"Thanks, Mom! Have a good day!" I hurried out of the house toward school. I looked at my watch as I opened the front door of our school, and I was amazed to see that it was only 7 A.M. I couldn't believe it; I was at school almost one whole hour early! I was sure Mrs. Mullins probably hadn't come yet. I headed for our class anyway.

When I got there, I saw that the lights were on, and Mrs. Mullins was writing on the board. "Wow! What time did you get here?" I asked.

Mrs. Mullins shrugged. "I couldn't sleep too well. I thought I would help your class get organized so everything could get done before the fair, you know." She was making lists of everything that we still had to do. I smiled to myself. Mrs. Mullins wanted to win!

I walked over toward the bathtub. "Maybe I should feed Mr. P. I'll just . . ." I looked into the tub and began to scream. Mrs. Mullins came rushing over. I just kept screaming. I couldn't stop. Finally, I gasped. "A leg. Look, a leg is growing out of Mr. P."

Mrs. Mullins looked in the tub, and together we stared at the piranha. It was having trouble swimming because just above the left fin, a small human-type leg stuck out. It looked sort of familiar, wearing jeans and a black boot. It was tiny but growing by the minute. Mr. P was turning into Mr. Monster-Sub Masters right before our eyes, "this . . . this," I croaked trying to find the words, "this is awful. I thought you said he couldn't change back for a week."

Mrs. Mullins looked at me, and she answered numbly, "It appears that I was wrong."

"Well," I said starting to pace. "We'll figure out something — eventually."

Mrs. Mullins glanced over at the clock, and my eyes followed hers. It was 7:15. The first kids would be getting to school in only a half hour. In the best circumstance, they would see Mr. Masters, and in the worst, they'd get half-fish, half-man. We were dead.

14

Mrs. Mullins moved away from the bathtub and sank down in the teacher's chair. "If only school weren't starting so soon. Maybe I could think of something."

I kept staring at the tank and with a sort of awful fascination, I watched the leg get a little bigger. We had to do something and quick. "Mrs. Mullins, I'll get the bucket. We'll dump in Mr. P or Mr. Masters or whatever he is and then . . . then we'll carry the bucket outside. We'll leave it somewhere behind the school where no one will notice." Everything was ruined as far as our class project. Jennifer was going to blame it all on me. It didn't matter. She couldn't know the truth. We couldn't let Mr. Masters turn from fish to man right in front of our whole class!

There was a little hope in Mrs. Mullins's eyes. "Okay," she said. "Hurry and get the bucket." I ran down to the janitor's closet praying it was unlocked! Thank goodness, it was, and I ran back with the bucket. When I got back into the class-room, Mrs. Mullins was peering into the tub. She straightened up. "Allan, I know how much you want to win the science fair. If we get Mr. P out of here, you lose any chance. Besides, you'll have to explain how he disappeared."

"But . . . if we don't get him out of here, every-one will know you're a witch. I'd rather lose the fair than lose you as my friend." I stuck out the bucket.

To my surprise, Mrs. Mullins hugged me. "Al-lan Hobart, we aren't beaten yet. I've been thinking while you were searching for that bucket. Maybe you don't have to give up the sci-ence fair, and I don't have to get discovered."

I looked at her and bit my lip. "But . . ."

She interrupted. "This piranha is turning back into Mr. Masters very slowly. If we try the spell just one more time with only a little of the pow-der, it ought to keep him a fish until the science fair is safely over." She peered at me over her granny glasses, and continued. "Can you run, and I do mean run, to my house and follow my di-rections exactly once you're there? If you can do that, and then hurry back before the other kids get here, we should be okay. Can you run that fast?"

I grabbed the paper, threw down the pail and tore out the door. If I didn't go fast enough . . . if any kid got in the room before I got back . . .

I couldn't stand to think of what happened next. I just went even faster. *Please don't let any teacher see me*, I thought as I ran down the hall. It was no time to get detention. I threw open the front door, and ran down the steps. "Young man, slow . . ." I heard far behind me, but instead, I forced my legs to pump harder. I pushed through the air with my hands, trying to get more speed. After one block, I could feel a sharp pain starting in my side. After three more, it hurt so bad I was having trouble breathing. But somehow, I made it to Mrs. Mullins's house. From my pocket, I pulled the emergency key she'd given me. My hands were shaking so badly that I had to use both of them to get the key in the door. At last, I flung it open and ran into the kitchen. It was the first time I'd ever opened Mrs. Mullins's spell potion cabinet, and even though I was in a terrible hurry, I shivered. The magic potions inside looked like hundreds of jars of flour. Quickly, I pulled from my pocket the name of the stuff Mrs. Mullins had to have. *Come on*, I told myself. *Find the right one fast!* I started reading labels. Darn! They weren't in alphabetical order. I knew I was taking too long, but I couldn't find the right potion. My hands started to shake even harder. *Come on, Allan*, I told myself. *Mrs. Mullins doesn't have time for you to take forever.*

At last, I saw the potion in the far-right corner of the cabinet. It was so far back that I'd almost missed it again. I opened the jar, grabbed some Saran Wrap, and poured the powder into the plastic wrap. I didn't even bother to put the jar back. I just jammed the powder-filled plastic into my pocket and ran back to the front door.

Locking it quickly, I took a deep breath and forced my legs to push hard back to school. Sweat was pouring off me, and my lungs felt like they were going to explode, but I knew I couldn't stop. Mrs. Mullins was risking everything for me and my school's science fair, and I had to get back fast.

I ran harder and faster than I had ever run in my life, but when I could see the playground, I knew that I hadn't been fast enough. There were lots of kids outside, which meant that kids had to be in our classroom, and they were probably standing around the bathtub seeing a fish and a leg like a miniature of Mr. Masters'. It was almost too awful to believe!

I knew I'd get caught by the playground monitor if I ran on the school grounds now, so I walked as fast as I could. My heart was pounding, and my hands were really shaking. I didn't know if it was because I'd run so hard, because I was terrified, or both. I race-walked my way down to room 5C, and as I got closer, I could tell that there were a bunch of kids standing outside the door. When I got closer, Jennifer said,

"Hurry up, it took you long enough! Did you get it?"

Get it? How could Jennifer know? "What do you . . ."

"Oh, Allan, now's not the time to be your dumb self. Mrs. Mullins is waiting! Go in before you ruin our whole project!"

"Okay," I said feeling totally baffled. "Okay, but . . ." Jennifer practically pushed me through the door.

"I wish I could come," she pouted as I pulled it shut behind me. When I got in the room, Mrs. Mullins was still leaning over the bathtub. I looked in and gasped. The piranha had two legs and two black boots now, and they were each about the size of my hand. I definitely recognized those boots from the beginning of the week when Mr. Masters had put his feet up on the desk.

I dug in my pocket and pulled out the packet. Mrs. Mullins whispered, "Oh, thank heavens!" She looked at me fiercely. "Now don't move a muscle. Don't whisper a word." With that she began her saying, blew a little magic powder on the piranha, and ended by firmly speaking the word FISH.

Just like that the legs and feet disappeared. The piranha looked all fish again. In fact, if anything he looked bigger and healthier than ever. Mrs. Mullins and I hugged each other. "Oh, my gosh," I exclaimed. "We actually did it!" I felt like my legs were going to give out right under me and I grabbed the nearest chair and plunked myself down in it. I shook my head trying to make sense of everything. "You . . . you didn't tell Jennifer what was happening, did you?"

Mrs. Mullins's eyes were gleaming. "Well I had to do something. You weren't back. The feet were definitely growing, and the children were starting to come into the room."

"So you told her?" I guess Mrs. Mullins could see how upset I was.

"Well, of course not. No one can share our secret."

"Then what did you say? Why are all those kids standing quietly outside our class door?"

Mrs. Mullins chuckled. "I told them that Mr. P was very ill, that I'd sent you for some medication, and that until we got the medicine in the water, any sudden movement in the room might kill Mr. P." Mrs. Mullins cleared her throat. "Actually, I believe it was Jennifer Swanson who volunteered to be the door guard and keep everyone out."

Mrs. Mullins looked at the fish tank again and grinned. "We're safe! No one knows about me, and the class project is ready to move on. We did it!" She stuck up her hand. "Give me five."

I grinned in spite of myself. I was the one who'd taught her that. We struck hands, and then I tried to stand up. I was too tired to move. There was a buzzing sound. "I think that's the bell," Mrs. Mullins said. "We'd better let everyone else inside."

Right, I tried to remind myself. School was just starting. We still had the whole day in front of us. I dragged myself back to my own seat, and Mrs. Mullins opened the door. "Good news, folks," she said. "The medicine seems to be working well. Have a look at Mr. P, and then sit down. We've lots to do."

Lots of kids commented that Mr. P looked fine. A couple said that he seemed even bigger, and after we sat down and heard the morning announcements, Candice leaned over and said, "How'd you know what to tell the vet? I'm glad they let you go. For sure, you'd be the one to get it down right." She smiled at me, and suddenly, I didn't feel quite so tired anymore.

Mrs. Mullins clapped her hands twice. "All right, here's what I've decided for today. Since there are no lesson plans, and since you got a late start on your project, and since you're learning a lot by doing it, I say we dedicate this day to making this room ready for everyone to have the best science fair that Miller Elementary School has ever seen!"

The whole class cheered, and everyone set to work. Mrs. Mullins didn't even have to remind us about our committees. Everyone knew where to go. We had only a few hours to make our room look like an aquarium. One group began to cover a wall with blue butcher paper. Another began to glue on fish, while two girls painted on a background of sea plants. Still another group was making a big poster about where piranhas were found. They said that the fish were mostly found in South American rivers. I guess that that group didn't know that piranhas lurked inside mean substitutes, too.

About 10:30 the fire alarm went off and, normally, we were all glad to hear it because it meant we got to go outside for a break, but today everyone groaned. "What a terrible day for a fire drill." Jennifer stamped her foot as if that would make it go away.

"Come, children, it might be a real fire. We have to leave the room," Mrs. Mullins instructed. I could swear she was getting to be just like a real teacher.

"Oh, I wouldn't worry about that," came Justin's voice from the back of the room.

"Justin, did you pull the fire alarm again?" Candice demanded.

"Who me?" Justin grinned wider. "I wouldn't do a thing like that. Can I help it if the rest of the school is going to sit outside waiting for the all-clear while we keep working."

Mrs. Mullins walked over to him, and shook a finger right at his face. "We don't need that kind of help to win. We'll just be the best because we are the best."

The day flew by. Mrs. Mullins said she'd eat her lunch in the room, and so most of us grabbed something to eat and came right back. At the end of the day, Principal Dugan came on the PA, "I want to wish every class the very best of luck in tonight's science fair. Come, bring your parents, your grandparents, and your friends. Be sure to be here at seven this evening, so you'll have time to stop by every room and see the wonderful things your fellow classmates have done. Now for a reminder about the judging. The judges will tour each room before the science fair starts, and we will announce the winners at seven-thirty. Good luck! See you all tonight!"

In room 5C, we heard the final bell ring, but no one left. Everyone was running around doing extra little things. Finally, almost an hour after school was out, we began cleaning up. When we were finished, we looked around the classroom. It didn't look like room 5C at all. One part of the room had huge charts explaining everything about piranhas. Another had a list of everyone's name in our class and a comment about what we had learned from this project. But my favorite was the whole section of the room that looked like an undersea paradise as good as *The Little Mermaid*. In the center of it all sat the bathtub with Mr. P. Candice had made a big sign that said

Mr. P WILL BE FED HIS DINNER AT 7:15. BE SURE TO STOP BY AND WATCH HIM EAT HIS LIVE GOLD-FISH. She put the sign next to the bathtub and giggled, "It's almost as if he knows he's the center of attention. Look at the way he flips his tail back and forth."

Justin said, "Hey, I want to be the one to feed him. I want to see him chop those sharp teeth right through those little goldfish."

"Gross," Amanda said.

"It's all part of the food chain," Jennifer announced in her best know-it-all voice.

"Well, it's still gross!" Amanda asserted.

"I think Allan should get to feed Mr. P. After all, we wouldn't even have him if it weren't for Allan," Candice said.

I gave her a big smile. I'd never noticed just how cute Candice was.

"Sounds fair to me," Jeff said.

Justin pouted. I thought for a minute. Jennifer was right; it was all part of the food chain, but Amanda was right, too; it was pretty gross to think of dropping those live goldfish in the water and watching Mr. P's sharp teeth sink into them. "You know, it's okay; Justin really wants to feed Mr. P, so he can."

"Really?" Justin looked at me like he was seeing me for the first time. "Hobart, you may even be okay!"

Finally, everything we could do was done. The

tables and chairs had all been pushed away from our displays, and Mrs. Mullins asked us to gather around the teacher's desk. "Look at this room. It is truly amazing. Would you recognize it as your classroom? Whether you win or not, you can be very proud of what you've done. Monday, when Mrs. Evans returns, she'll be most impressed with the kids in room five-C."

Amanda said, "I wish you could be our teacher all the time." A lot of kids nodded, and I felt so proud of my friend.

Mrs. Mullins's eyes sparkled. "Thanks, it's definitely been a most memorable week. But trust me, I know that it's best for you *and for me* that Mrs. Evans is taking over." I didn't say anything, but I was sure that school would never be nearly as exciting again. After all, Mrs. Evans probably had no idea how to turn people into fish.

Justin piped up, "Well, are we outta here?"

Mrs. Mullins chuckled, "We're outta here! See you all tonight at the school's science fair."

15

I was so excited about the science fair that I forgot all about Mrs. Mullins's dress, or rather the lack of her dress, for her tea tomorrow until I got home. I called her. "I'm sorry. I thought we would have time to work on your dress today."

"Oh, that's okay. Allan, I have a beautiful dress. It's just perfect!"

"You do?" I was glad and all, but I felt sort of bad that she'd done the spell without me.

"Yes! The ladies at the tea will be impressed. It's better than anything I could have ever invented."

I twisted the phone cord. "Uh . . . so you didn't make magic to get it."

"No . . . well, maybe, well yes . . . well, actually, Agatha Eloise sent it."

I was totally confused. "Uh . . . who's Agatha Eloise?"

"Oh, she's a friend of mine in Boston. About two o'clock today, I started thinking of her and wishing she could be here. She always used spells to make the most beautiful things. Her recipes always turned out right."

I twisted the cord some more. "So, you called her, and she had a dress . . ."

Mrs. Mullins laughed. "Oh, no, Allan. I had no time to call. I was in class with you all day. I just thought about it really hard, and when I got home, the dress was waiting in my living room, along with the recipe for making it!"

I gulped. "You mean it was like ESP?"

"Exactly," she bubbled. "I can't often get it to work. Most of the time, I think about things, and nothing happens, but today, the airwaves were just right. Oops, I hear a car horn. That must be your mom picking me up for dinner. See you soon."

I put down the phone. This ESP thing could be pretty neat. Imagine wishing some genius could take my math homework and *poof* it would be done.

It was only a few minutes until I heard the door open, and my mom called, "Hi! I took off early. I didn't want you to be late for the school's science fair. I stopped and picked up some Big Macs on the way." She opened the hamburger bag, put some catsup on the table for the fries, poured me a glass of milk, and Mrs. Mullins a glass of tea.

As we ate, I gave Mom the basic details, minus of course, the morning's beginning when we'd found Mr. P growing legs. She said that she couldn't wait to see what we had done because it sounded as if our room looked wonderful. Mom looked at Mrs. Mullins, "Henrietta, from what I hear, you've done a wonderful job with the children this week. How lucky we all are that you've moved here. Right, Allan?"

"Absolutely," I said.

In no time, dinner was over, and we were on our way to school. We pulled into the parking lot which was already jammed with cars. Mom had to drive around it three times before she finally found a parking space. She parked the car, and we went in the building. "Let's go to my room first," I said. "I want to make sure everything is okay, and then we'll go see our competition." As we walked down the hall, I could hardly believe that this was the same place I was tearing through so fast only this morning trying to get the right potion. Our classroom was very full. It seemed like the whole school was there. I edged my way through to make sure that nothing weird was going on with Mr. P, and then I headed back for the door. Two parents were talking to Mrs. Mullins, telling her how wonderful she was. My mom was talking to Jennifer Swanson's mom, so I headed out the door to see the other classes on my own.

The first grades had all joined together to do

a dinosaur unit. I guess it was good for first-graders, but it wasn't too exciting. They just had pictures they had drawn, and scrawled sentences on fat lined paper about their drawings. One fourth grade had made a pretty interesting volcano. When they put some stuff into it, the volcano blew out smoke and stuff. It was neat. Mrs. Johnson's sixth-grade project on bees turned out to be dumb. After seeing every room, I thought our toughest competition came from Mrs. Angor's sixth grade. They had this whole thing about chemistry. They had lots of charts with chemicals and models of stuff that they had made. It was boring, but it looked like the kind of stuff teacher-judges would think was smart. Mr. Sweeny's third grade had turtles, but no other class had any live animals, and turtles didn't begin to compare to a real piranha.

I headed back to our room which had gotten even more crowded. "It's time to feed the piranha," Justin shouted over the crowd. He really hammed it up. He took the wiggling goldfish out of a small bowl, held it up high, and opened his own mouth as if he was going to toss it in, then instead of putting it in his mouth, he dropped the squirming little goldfish into the bathtub. Those people close enough to the piranha gasped as Mr. P ate his dinner.

At 7:30 we all went to the auditorium. Principal Dugan talked about the reason for the fair;

he introduced all the judges. He went on and on and on. He announced third place which went to the first-graders and their dinosaurs. Second place went to Mrs. Angor's sixth-grade class. There were a few gasps at that. I heard a kid behind me whisper. "We've got it. The fourth-grade volcano had to win first."

Then Mr. Dugan said, "And the first-place winner for this science fair is . . ." he paused and the room was totally silent. "Room five-C and their piranha project!"

We all cheered. Mr. Dugan waited for quiet and then talked about how not only was our project outstanding in every aspect, but that he was particularly impressed that we had been able to do it even with our teacher gone and a change of substitutes midweek. He went on to say how our project showed that Miller Elementary School had prepared its students to be creative thinkers ready to face any problem. We rolled our eyes. Leave it to Principal Dugan to take credit!

Finally, Mr. Dugan invited our class chairman to come forward and accept the blue ribbon and the certificate for the class pizza party. We all looked around at each other. We'd been too busy to ever even think about a class chairman. Everything just sort of stopped. Then Justin started to walk up, but Candice's voice rang out to stop him. "Actually Mr. Dugan, we didn't really elect a chairman; we just all worked together. But if it hadn't been for Allan Hobart bringing the piranha in and Mrs. Mullins staying after and helping us work, we wouldn't have had any project at all."

Mr. Dugan cleared his throat. "Fine. Then Mrs. Mullins and Allan, why don't you come up and get the blue ribbon." I walked toward the front of the auditorium and up on the stage. All the parents started to stand up and clap. It was amazing. Me, Allan, who felt invisible most of the time up here getting a standing ovation. I wished this minute would never end.

But, of course, it did. The assembly was over. Mom had tears in her eyes. She told me how proud I had made her, and she started to hug me, but I moved away before anyone saw! Lots of kids came up to read our certificate about the pizza party. Finally, everyone started to clear out. Mom was talking to some lady over in one corner. Mrs. Mullins and I walked over to her. "Allan, Mrs. Mullins, this is Louise Thompson. We went to school together. I haven't seen her in years. She's just in visiting her sister who has a daughter in third grade here."

Mrs. Thompson congratulated us on winning and said, "I was absolutely bewitched by your project!"

My eyes got big. "You were?" I questioned.

Mrs. Mullins nudged me. "Thank you. It was fun to help the children this week."

I figured I had better get out of there before I put my foot in my mouth really bad. "Mom, as long as you're still talking, can I go back to the room once more? We'll have to take everything apart as soon as school starts on Monday, and I want to see it all just the way it is one more time."

Half the lights went out in the auditorium. Mom said, "I think they want us out of here. But I'll tell you what. It's so lovely that Louise and I will chat right outside the front door of school, and you can come get me when you're done in your room. Don't be too long. I think they want to lock up soon." Mrs. Mullins and I went back to room 5C. When we got there, the janitor was just turning off the lights in the room. Mrs. Mullins told him she would take care of the lights and shut the door when we left. The janitor shrugged. "Okay by me. Hey, pretty amazing fish you've got there. What are you gonna do with him anyway?"

"Uh?" I said.

Mrs. Mullins jumped in. "Oh, we'll probably return him to where we got him."

The janitor left. Mrs. Mullins and I headed toward the bathtub. "Uh, when," I said, "when do you think, he'll, you know . . . he'll turn back into Mr. Masters?"

"Well," she said, "I imagine it will be some time around Saturday afternoon. But I'm absolutely sure he won't still be here on Monday."

We peered into the tub to get a good look at our piranha. "Well," I said to him, "you came through after all Mr. Monster-Sub. You helped our class win the school's science fair."

Mr. P, soon to be Mr. Masters, was swimming real fast back and forth around the tub. It was almost like he knew he wasn't going to be able to swim much longer. "What do you think will happen when he turns back into himself, and he . . . he finds out?"

Mrs. Mullins shook her head. "Oh, Mr. Masters will never know. He'll just be surprised to find himself sitting fully dressed in a bathtub in the front of the classroom."

I tilted my baseball cap back. "Boy, I wish I could see that!"

Mrs. Mullins looked at me over her granny glasses. "Really? With his temper, you'd want to be the one he sees first?"

"Well, maybe not," I said. "Everyone is sure going to be surprised when they come in on Monday and the piranha is gone. What do I tell them?"

"The truth," Mrs. Mullins said.

"The truth?" I questioned. "But . . ."

Mrs. Mullins interrupted. "When you left him on Friday night, he was swimming around in his tank, right?"

"Uh-huh," I said.

Mrs. Mullins walked to the classroom door. "I think it's time for us to go find your mother." She pulled the door shut behind us, but she didn't close it all the way. "Come with me," she said.

"Uh, Mrs. Mullins, the front door and my mom are the other direction."

She smiled. "Oh, I know that. But I think perhaps we'd better leave one school door a bit ajar. After all, we don't want Mr. Masters to still be pacing the halls on Monday morning."

"Right." We put a small stick in the back door to the school because we knew that the janitor had already checked it. I said, "I still wish I could stay to see it all happen. Couldn't we just hide in a closet or something?"

Mrs. Mullins started back toward the auditorium. "I think we've pressed our luck quite enough, thank you. Let's find your mother and go home. I've got a tea to go to tomorrow. You've got a pizza party to plan when you get back here on Monday. That will have to do for excitement."

When we got outside the front door, it wasn't hard to spot my mom and her old friend. Everyone else was gone. Mom said good-bye to her friend and we started walking to the car. Mrs. Mullins and Mom got in the front seat. I climbed in the back, and watched through the window as we pulled away from school. My mom switched on the radio. "What a lovely evening," she said. "You both should be so proud of yourselves. I

148

know I'm certainly proud of you. It was all very exciting." We drove a little farther, and Mom added almost to herself, "Imagine my seeing Louise again after all this time. Isn't it amazing what surprises a day can bring."

I thought of the way this day had begun and ended. "It sure is," I said.

16

I put the big blue ribbon in my room when we got home. Then happy and exhausted, I went to bed. Saturday, I checked my room tons to look at the ribbon again. On Monday, it would belong to the class, but it was mine for this weekend. It was the last thing I saw before I went to sleep Saturday night.

Sunday morning, I woke with a start. I rubbed my eyes and looked at the clock by my bed. The digital numbers read 4:55. My heart was pounding so hard that it felt as if it was going to thump right out of my chest. I decided I must have had some kind of a nightmare. I sat up in bed, but all I could remember was that there had been something really scary. Then the terrible dream started to come back. It was Monday morning. Mrs. Evans had returned. The bathtub was still in the front of the room, but . . . so was Mr. Masters or Mr. P. He was part-man, part-fish, and everyone in our class was shouting. Suddenly, the fish was gone, and our monster-sub looked even meaner than his usual mean self. He roared at the kids and Mrs. Evans. He asked who had done this terrible thing to him.

Jennifer pointed and called, "It was Allan Hobart. He said he brought the piranha in for our class project. Him and his baby-sitter." Mr. Masters snarled, and his huge black boots began to pound their way toward my desk.

I took a deep breath. I told myself this was only a dream. Not real. None of it could really happen. It was just my imagination. Mr. Masters would be long gone before Monday. Mrs. Mullins was sure of it.

I started to feel a little better. I lay back down in bed. My heart stopped pounding quite so hard. Then I carefully considered my friend. Her magic almost never worked exactly the way she planned. She'd said that her original formula would keep Mr. Masters a fish for a week, but it hadn't. What if this formula left him a fish for longer than she thought. Could there be a part-man, part-fish swimming around on Monday? It was entirely possible. I decided I had to know.

Very quietly, so I wouldn't wake my mom, I put on my jeans and a sweatshirt, laced on my shoes, and pulled my hat down over my hair. I'd be back before Mom was ever up. That way I wouldn't have to answer any questions. I would get to school and slip in through the back door that we'd left open. If the tub was empty, fine. If it wasn't, well . . . well first I'd find out if it was empty.

I left my house and headed toward school. The streetlights were still on. I didn't plan to stop at Mrs. Mullins, but her house was right on the way, and when I went past it, I found myself walking up to her front door and ringing the bell. I guess I didn't quite want to face monster-man by myself. I rang and rang the doorbell. Mrs. Mullins finally came to the door. She had on a long red flannel nightgown, and there was some kind of weird hair net on her head. "Good heavens!" she said. "What are you doing here? It's still the middle of the night. What's wrong?"

I told her. At first, she replied that I should quit worrying, go home, and go back to bed. "I told you that the spell would end in time," she said yawning.

I reminded her about our other spells. Her ending up shocking pink, Himself the elf, and the fact that Mr. Masters was not supposed to have started turning from fish to man on Friday. She looked at me for a minute, said she'd be right back, and came out dressed. We walked to school in the early morning light, cold and nervous about what we might find.

I had never been at school on a Sunday at 5:30 in the morning. It was weird, and it was even weirder to sneak in through the open back door.

"He'll be gone, you'll see," Mrs. Mullins said, but I didn't know if she was telling me or trying to convince herself.

I put my hand on the knob of room 5C, made myself open the door, and walk into the classroom. "Uhh, ohh, uhh . . ." I tried to say words to Mrs. Mullins, but no words would come out. I couldn't talk, and I couldn't move my feet. Then Mrs. Mullins grabbed my hand, and she pulled me into the coat closet in the back of the room. Peeking out, we saw long jeans-clad legs standing in the bathtub. We saw a soggy white shirt with muscles bulging out of it, and we saw big man's hands reaching up to touch . . . the head of a piranha!

Then from our hidden spot, we watched as the head of the fish slowly started to transform itself into that of a man with a big black mustache. Right before our eyes, the fish disappeared, and Mr. Masters came back. The very last thing to return were his coal-black piercing eyes. His face contorted in anger and confusion as those eyes looked down and saw that he was standing in a bathtub of water in front of the classroom. "What the *#4*%*&^%##@#$%^%^T%$R^%^^ %$#$###$$!" I was sure that those words had never been said in room 5C before. Mrs. Mullins and I scrunched back into the closet a little further. He looked mad enough to kill whomever he found.

Mr. Masters stepped out of the bathtub; then his big hand reached up to scratch his chin. His voice boomed into the silence, "How'd I get in a bathtub in an empty room?" He shook his head. "Why can't I remember?"

His black eyes glared at the empty desks. "Kids," he spat the word. "I hate 'em. I hate their sniveling little smiles. I hate their stupid little questions." He looked back at the tub for a minute. "No one ever gets the best of me." He hitched his thumbs through his belt and his voice rang throughout the room. "Tough luck, little kiddies; someone else is going to have to straighten out all you spoiled little lamebrains. I've got better things to do. I'm not subbing here or anywhere ever again!"

His big black boots strode across the room angrily. He yanked open the door to the classroom, and we heard him pulling at the front door to get out of the school. Then he cussed some more and we heard his boots pound in the hallway as he headed for the back door. Then all was quiet.

Mrs. Mullins and I stayed in the closet for quite a while. We weren't taking any chances. Finally, when we were sure he must have left, we walked out and took a last look at the empty tub. I was excited. "He's gone! No one will ever have to know the truth about our piranha! Mrs. Mullins, did you hear Mr. Masters? He isn't ever going to substitute again. No kids will ever have to undergo the monster-sub and his awfulness again. Wow! Thanks!"

"It was no problem." Mrs. Mullins said and she stuck out her hand to give me a high five, "All it took was a little fifth-grade magic."

About the Author

Terri Fields lives in Phoenix, Arizona, with her husband, Rick, and her children, Lori and Jeffrey. A teacher who believes there are always magical mysteries at home and in school, she's also the author of *The Day the Fifth Grade Disappeared*, *Bug Off!*, and *Fourth-Graders Don't Believe in Witches*.